"Tell me again why you're interviewing for husbands?" Cole prodded.

Her cutting glare could have drawn blood from a lesser man. Even Cole felt its jab. She turned away. "Oh, right," he drawled. "It's that career move. What job could be so all-fired important that you'd make this mad dash to snag a husband?"

"You have some nerve!" She kneaded her temples as though trying to ward off a headache. "You don't know me! You don't have any right to presume anything about me!"

"I know plenty of women like you. Only a guy with nothing going on between the ears would agree to some half-baked marriage scheme."

"Then you'd be perfect for the job!" she cried, her eyes a blink away from tears.

"So where do I get in line?" That crazy question came out of nowhere. The shock on her face was no more staggering than the shock Cole felt from hearing the inquiry in his own voice.

BRIDEGROOM ON HER DOORSTEP

Renee Roszel

You are invited to a

WHITE WEDDING

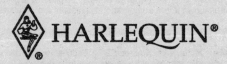

HARLEQUIN®

TORONTO • NEW YORK • LONDON
AMSTERDAM • PARIS • SYDNEY • HAMBURG
STOCKHOLM • ATHENS • TOKYO • MILAN • MADRID
PRAGUE • WARSAW • BUDAPEST • AUCKLAND

To:
Doug and Randy
How about a hug?

ISBN 0-373-03725-2

BRIDEGROOM ON HER DOORSTEP

First North American Publication 2002.

CHAPTER ONE

WHAT caught Jennifer Sancroft's eye—and her breath—wasn't the majestic view of the Gulf of Mexico. It was the powerful flex of muscle in the stranger's back and shoulders, even two hundred feet away impressively conspicuous. She noticed him immediately. Tall, tanned and shirtless, he slathered white paint on a picket fence separating a manicured lawn from a pristine beach.

Her engine coughed and the car shuddered. Forcing her gaze away from the hunky vision, Jen turned off the engine of her mid-size rental car. Now that she no longer looked at the man, her brain let her in on the complication he could present. "How am I supposed to hold discreet interviews for a husband with some blue-collar hunk lurking around?"

Ruthie Tuttle, Jen's assistant, had pushed open her car door and leaned halfway out. With Jen's muttered comment she hunched back inside and turned around. "Did you say something, boss?"

Jen shook her head. "No, I was thinking out loud." She indicated the bare-chested man in the distance. "I hope he was only hired for the weekend. I don't need anybody scaring away my applicants."

Ruthie glanced in the direction of her boss's wave, her serious expression changing to curiosity, then fascination. Her lips parted in a silent "Oh" that spoke volumes.

"Well, well..." Ruthie finally said, with a lewd grin. Jen had never seen such a lustful expression on her assistant's freckled face. Annoyed with herself for feeling exactly the way Ruthie looked, she lightly elbowed the woman in the ribs, prodding her out of fantasyland.

"*Tuttle!* You have a perfectly nice husband. Close your mouth!''

Ruthie cleared her throat, her violet gaze sliding to her boss. "Just 'cause I'm tied to the porch, doesn't mean I can't bark!'' She looked at the painter, her gaze lingering. "Didn't I mention the leasing agent said there might be a maintenance guy on the property?''

"No," Jen said, experiencing a rush of aggravation. "You did not.''

"Oops." Ruthie's grin refused to dim as she surveyed the stranger. "Just between you and me, he is a great example of *prime* guy maintenance!''

Jen glowered at her assistant. So what if he was prime? That didn't make him any *less* of an impediment to her plans. She shifted her gaze away to stare, unseeing, at her hands, clutching the steering wheel. Why couldn't things ever run smoothly? The corporation-owned property she'd rented for the next three weeks was somewhat isolated for her peace of mind, but beggars couldn't be choosers, and this was the only property available. The accounting firm's presidency had opened up so abruptly, she'd been forced to make some quick—possibly even rash—decisions.

She didn't dare hold husband interviews in Dallas. The word would surely get back to the firm that she wasn't actually on her honeymoon. Exposed as a liar, she would lose her chance at the top job of the conservative firm— not to mention she would be so disgraced she'd have to leave the state to find a job!

No! She wouldn't let that happen! She'd worked too long and hard for Dallas Accounting Associates, given the company her body and her soul for a decade. She deserved the presidency. To get it, she planned to move heaven and earth if she had to!

"That painter had better not get in my way," she muttered. "I have less than a month to find, and marry, an appropriate husband. I don't need some hulking hired hand stomping all over my timetable in his size-twelve boots!''

She looked at her assistant, a stocky, curly top, ex-marine. "I might have to sic you on him, Tuttle."

Ruthie gave a quick, surprised laugh. "He's pretty big, boss. I'll need more marines." She pressed her lips together and frowned as though having a dark thought. "Or I could call my in-laws to come on down and join us. They could chase *anybody* away." She grinned wryly. "Case in point, if my mother and father-in-law—or as I like to refer to them, the Wicked Witch of Wichita Falls and Toad-man— hadn't decided to invade the happy Tuttle abode for an extended visit, you'd never have talked me into taking three whole weeks away from Ray and the kids." She shook her head and eyed heaven. "Considering the thousands of my-son-could-have-done-*much*-better glares you saved me from suffering through, boss, I owe you *big*."

Jen unclenched a fist from the wheel and patted her assistant's arm. "Let's call it even, Ruthie. I need your ability to keep a schedule and a confidence." She took a quick scan of the place, on the secluded stretch of beach. "Considering we're so isolated here, and considering I'll practically be propositioning a steady stream of single, heterosexual men, I might need your proficiency in the martial arts." Jen unlatched her door and stepped onto the gravel drive. "Speaking of men, I'm going to find out what's what with that painter." She slammed the car door and marched across the lawn toward her quarry.

Concentrating on the tall stranger who seemed oblivious to the fact that she'd driven up, Jen tromped toward him. As she stormed along the lawn, she hardly noticed the two-story brick house with its white trim, or the window boxes brimming with red geraniums. She tramped past a white cottage trimmed in blue, off to her left. More window boxes, overflowing with vivid reds, yellows and greens, went virtually unseen.

Jen was by nature a positive, confident and logical person. At the moment, however, she was less than her usual efficient self. She was on a tight timetable and more than a little angry. She would not be passed over for the promotion she deserved! Not this time! The tang of the sea rode in on the breeze but went virtually unnoted. Jen's senses were wholly focused on the all-important task ahead of her. It was going to be difficult enough to do what she had to do *without* an audience. Ruthie could be trusted, but the stranger was a major question mark.

A six-and-a-half-foot-tall question mark!

Tension intensified her hostility for this outsider who dared intrude on her secret itinerary. It was bad enough that Ruthie had to know. Putting up with her sidelong looks of disapproval was plenty to deal with. She didn't need some stranger blundering around in her private business. She didn't think she could cope with one more person looking at her like she was a fool or worse—crazy.

It was nobody's business how she found a mate but her own! She'd trusted her heart once and fallen madly in love with...

Tony.

She stumbled at the recollection, but caught herself. Even after four years it still hurt just to *think* his name.

Tony Lund had been hired at Dallas Accounting Associates as her immediate superior. From the first time the elevator doors opened and he'd stepped onto her floor, she had been lost. He was handsome, suave, brilliant, with a mystical way of knowing exactly what to say to make her feel wonderful. Even his casual smiles as they passed in the hallway sent her into fits of dizzy euphoria.

It had taken six months for Jen to catch Tony's eye—as a woman rather than a mere work colleague. That magical moment had come at the company Christmas party. She'd taken excessive pains with her clothes, at last dressing for a man rather than for success. She'd had her hair restyled and highlighted and devoured makeup hints in slick women's magazines. Before Tony she'd been completely preoccupied with her career; suddenly she found herself giddily playing all the feminine games to get Tony to notice her. By Christmas he had a reputation for being a lady's man, but Jen hated gossip and ignored the stories.

New Year's Eve had been their first official date. Tony was the epitome of gentlemanly, and was worldly enough to sense her reticence at moving too quickly to intimacy. After all, he was her boss, though there were no strict rules against dating a co-worker. Jen loved her job, or had loved it until a newer, brighter love swept into her life.

Tony.

Even with her concern about getting physically involved too quickly, one month after they'd begun to date, Tony confessed his love for her. Though ultra-conservative and cautious, Jen was on the brink of giving up everything for him that she'd held so dear—her career and her virginity.

Feeling cherished and desired, Jen dwelled in a perpetual pink haze of love. All she wanted in the world was to be Tony's wife and the mother of his children.

On Valentine's Day, Jen had been the happiest woman in Texas. Wearing a new dress she could hardly afford, she felt like a giddy teenager. She'd been ready for Tony to pick her up for what she knew would be a romantic, life-changing evening, when the phone rang.

It was her mother, tearfully calling from a Fort Worth hospital. Jen's favorite Aunt Crystal had been in a car accident and was in a critical condition. Rushing to the hospital, distraught and in tears, Jen caught Tony on his cell phone and canceled their date. He'd offered to come to the hospital, but she'd told him it wasn't necessary.

That Valentine's Day ended tragically when Jen's aunt passed away. Deep in the night, broken up with grief, Jen found herself driving back to Dallas toward Tony's apartment, needing his comfort and closeness. She had made the decision to give him her most precious gift, her unqualified, physical love—an affirmation of life. She would be his completely, and he would be hers—lovers, soul mates, forever.

When he met her at the door, she knew immediately

something wasn't right. Bare-chested, in black, silk pajama bottoms, he smiled that magical smile. Even bleary with sleep he was godlike in his perfection. Yet, something in his eyes frightened her. Intuition made her brush past him and head for his bedroom, dreading what she would find.

When Jen burst into the room, another woman sat up in bed, fumbling to cover her bare breasts. As the two women stared at each other, Tony grabbed Jen's arm, whispering it didn't mean anything. "It just happened," he'd said, his expression more sheepish than repentant, as though suggesting that these overnight seductions were of no consequence.

She recalled so vividly, with such stark pain, how he'd swung her into his arms, managing somehow to cleverly maneuver her out of the bedroom and close the door. How smooth he was, even caught *flagrante delicto!*

He'd murmured that he loved her and that "It was only sex," all the time smiling and softly cajoling, his tongue in her ear. What a resilient cheat he was!

In a twilight world of the brokenhearted, she had stood there, crushed. The man she'd almost given herself to was cleverly and cold-bloodedly plying his wiles while a casual sexual conquest lay in his bed on the other side of a door, wholly forgotten.

She pushed away from him, staring in disgust and disbelief at his perplexed expression. He didn't even have the decency to recognize his betrayal. Her heart had gone down, literally sank as she grieved to the depths of her soul. She had been so irrationally in love she'd allowed herself to be blinded to his lies, evasions, infidelities, no matter how often her friends had tried to warn her.

That night Jen endured two very painful deaths—a beloved member of her family, and her desire to ever again be caught up in the thick, mind-clogging pink fog called love! She had been out of control once, and it shattered her. *Never again!*

Tony had the nerve to call her several times after that,

his silver-tongued vows of devotion seemingly ardent and heartfelt. Though Jen suffered the tortures of the damned, she resisted falling for his sly charm. Two endless months passed. Months of enduring his presence at work, his casual touches and melting looks, those warm, hazel eyes—eyes that softly tempted, promising never to lie, even as they lied. Eyes that could drive a sane woman mad and turn an intelligent one into a fool.

Tony's cunningly subtle come-ons at the office became almost too persuasive to resist. Jen began to fear for her sanity and her resolve to resist him. Then, as suddenly as he had come, Tony left D.A.A., his natural charisma and business acumen landing him a splendid position in New York City's financial district.

Tony was too aggressive, too commanding to be content to remain at a small, conservative firm like D.A.A. As his final *coup de grâce,* proving his ruthless amorality, he eloped with a co-worker, someone he had surely been making love to even as he'd sweet-talked Jen, attempting to destroy her resolve. His unlucky, deluded bride wasn't even the same woman she'd caught him in bed with!

Sadly, Jen found the pain and sense of betrayal did not diminish after Tony's departure from her life. His easy, unapologetic and persistent breaches of faith taught her an agonizing lesson. Tony had not been the only betrayer in this. She had also been betrayed by the treachery of her own emotions, allowing her to be so blind and deaf to the man's true, black character. *Never again would she let her emotions run riot.*

Logic and intellect became her watchwords. After Tony was gone, Jen threw herself into her career, reestablishing it as supremely important in her life, and she'd risen rapidly through the ranks at D.A.A. Any desire to attract a man with physical trappings, like sexy clothes or makeup, was gone, crushed with her naiveté.

The presidency of D.A.A. would be hers, this time, or she would die trying! She knew from unhappy experience the company was severely conservative. The presidency had always gone to, and would always go to, a settled, married man. Though she could do nothing about her gender, Jennifer Sancroft was determined to mold herself into the perfect presidential candidate—which required an immediate and respectable mate.

This husband hunt she'd hurriedly put into motion would be conducted on a strictly analytical basis. She would not let emotions blind her and open her up to pain.

Never again.

She would play it safe, be in total control. She would secure for herself a mate who was not only successful in his own right, but who shared her interests and beliefs. Finding a life's partner with intellect instead of insubstantial and untrustworthy hormone-induced emotion was certainly possible. Her own parents were the perfect example of a well-oiled team with like minds who had never been slobbery over each other. Jen simply needed a plan, a few good candidates, and some privacy—which at the moment was the subject at hand.

She marched down the sloping lawn, her attention riveted on the man painting the fence. When she was within stone-throwing distance, he startled her by glancing in her direction. His features were as grim as hers, as though her approach had not been a surprise.

Before she reached him, he laid his brush across the paint can and straightened, bracing his hands on his hips. His unfriendly expression suggested *she* was the one intruding. *Well!* He had some nerve! Just who was the executive and who was the hireling?

She thought she detected the flare of his nostrils. "So you're the tenant." He sounded as though he'd expected her but would not have grieved extravagantly if she'd driven off a cliff.

"Yes, I am." Her aggravated tone matched his. "When will you be finished with your chores? *This weekend*, I trust, because Monday morning I begin some very important—meetings, and I can't have a lot of banging and—and—*whatever*…'' She waved away the rest of the sentence. Of all people, a maintenance man would know what noises a maintenance man made.

He remained silent, his skeptical examination giving off insolent vibes. Even as annoyed as his cheeky impudence made her, a corner of her brain whispered that he had an amazing face. His eyes were an otherworldly pale, spectacular, almost hypnotic. Though she assumed their color was a very light blue, in the bright June sun, they exhibited an iridescence reminding her of fire opals. Staring into them she lost her train of thought as well as a fraction of her animosity.

His striking eyes narrowed, masked by a dark frill of lashes. He pursed his lips for a beat, then shrugged. The movement caused a sinewy ripple across his chest. ''I can't do much about the banging, but I'll try to keep the whatever down.''

She scowled, confused. What was he talking about? She met his eyes, not realizing until that moment that her gaze had strayed lower. Her cheeks grew hot and she feared she might be blushing. ''Excuse me?'' The snapped inquiry came out breathier than she would have preferred.

He inhaled, nostrils flaring again, drawing her attention to the symmetry of his straight patrician nose and how nicely it fitted above a handsome, if cynically twisted, mouth. Her gaze traveled down again, and she took conspicuous notice of his square chin, bisected by a sexy cleft.

''Look, Miss…'' As he paused, she shook off her odd preoccupation, mentally scrambling to regain focus on why she'd confronted him.

Before continuing his thought, he leaned slightly forward. If he were anyone else Jen wouldn't have noticed, but he was so—so big. The move unsettled her and she took a step backward. ''Whether you like it or not,'' he said, ''I'm here for the month of June. The leasing agent made a mistake.'' He gave her a curt but brazen once-over.

"Since you're a woman who, by your own admission, has an aversion to *banging,* I suggest you make other arrangements."

She stared at him, hoping his remark had no underlying sexual content. Surely not. He couldn't have the mental dexterity to juggle a double entendre. "What do you mean by *mistake?*" she asked.

His brow wrinkled at her question. "I mean the usual—error, blunder, oversight, slip—"

"I understand the word!" she cut in. "I mean, *what* mistake?"

"The corporation never rents this property in June."

"Of course it does," she said. "I'm here, aren't I?"

"That was the mistake."

She had a sinking feeling, but didn't respond.

"Your being allowed to rent the place was a mistake," he said.

Refusing to take his word, she demanded, "Why should I believe you?"

"Call and ask."

Not one to be bullied, she whipped her cell phone from her shoulder bag and punched in the corporate headquarters' number.

"It's Saturday," he said.

She realized what he meant, scowled at him and snapped her cell phone shut. "Right." Disconcerted, she slipped the phone into the bag, working to regain her self-assurance. "Look, I don't care what day it is. I've leased this place for the next three weeks, so that's that."

His dark, lustrous hair fluttered appealingly, ruffled by the fingertips of a sea breeze. An ebony curl fell across his creased brow, cavorted there for a few heartbeats, then dashed up to rejoin the dark waves of his hair. Troubled by the way that dancing wisp affected her, she shifted her attention to his scintillating gaze and experienced a jolt when their eyes met.

"For years, June has been set aside for m..." His jaw

bunched. "...maintenance. Apparently the new leasing manager isn't on the ball."

His revelation penetrated. From the hostile conviction glittering in his eyes, she felt renewed misgivings.

"This isn't going to work," he said.

"It has to work," she countered. "I've made *arrangements*. I have appointments scheduled all next week. Some of the—my applicants are coming from out of state. My advertisement runs through next week and gives *this* address. I can't possibly change my plans!"

"Neither can I."

Jen detected no hint of concern or apology in the statement. If anything there had been a knife edge of resentment in his tone. If his sparking stare was any indicator, he was far from sympathetic to her predicament.

She adjusted her shoulders to make sure she stood as erect as her five-foot-six frame would muster. The difference in their dimensions was still laughably one-sided. If he took it in his head, he could squash her like a jelly doughnut. Judging by his expression, he was poised on the verge.

Unwilling to let his hostility cow her, she met him scowl for scowl. This guy had never come up against Jennifer Sancroft when she had set a goal. "Then..." she said, keeping her voice composed, "it looks like we're at an impasse."

He glared for a long moment, then surprising her, he nodded. "That's how it looks."

Jen didn't like compromise, especially with someone who should have been easy to deal with. She'd misjudged this hunky hulk. She'd thought he'd fold, groveling and begging her pardon. Apparently he took his time schedule as seriously as she took hers. Maybe reshuffling this job to a later date would mean having to cancel something else, which would take a bite out of his livelihood. Being a logical person, she could understand his obstinacy, if allowing

her to force him off the property would steal bread from
his family's table.

Jen's turn had come to shrug. Maybe she was being para-
noid. It wasn't likely that a Texas coast handyman's gos-
siping would get all the way to a Dallas accounting firm.
Besides, looking at that set jaw, she sensed he wasn't the
gossipy type. She had enough to worry about without getting overly mistrustful. "Well, I suppose…" The sentence
died from lack of enthusiasm. With effort, she forged on,
facing the fact she didn't have a choice. "I guess—you can
stay. I only ask that you don't bang around inside the house
while I'm—I'm interviewing." She met his hard, pale gaze.
"You'll keep your distance. Agreed?"

Even filled with animosity his brilliant, fire-opal eyes
were awe-inspiring. After a silent interlude that seemed like
a year, his head dipped in a slow, begrudging half nod.

Cole glowered at the woman standing before him, stunned
to realize he'd actually agreed to any concession. His plan
had been to grab whoever showed up by the scruff of the
neck and haul him bodily out to the highway. What had it
been about this female that made him change his mind? Or
more correctly, *lose* it?

Frowning at her, he took in the tailored suit. The muddy
cotton broadcloth, cut to make her look like she wore two
cardboard boxes, thoroughly hid any evidence of her femininity. And that hair. Parted in the center, she'd slicked it
back into a tight twist at her nape. She might as well wear
a sign that read I Am A Dowdy, Finicky Virgin. Approach
At Your Own Risk.

Unfortunately for his plans, her glistening eyes told a
different story. They were large, shiny. The lids rode low
over the most vibrant green he'd ever seen. Her slumberous
lids and a sweep of sooty-brown lashes whispered sly se-
ductiveness. The come-hither sensation, however unwit-
tingly given, was impossible to ignore. Then there was her
mouth. Those lips had a pouty way about them that, even

amid all that muddy-brown fabric and skinned-back hair, gave off a stirring eroticism.

He had the strong sense the sexiness of those cupid's bow lips was unintentional, unlike most of the women he'd brushed up against in his life—designing femme fatales angling for personal gain. But not this one. She hadn't come on to him. Far from it. That fact alone—the "I'm sexy but I'll never tell" vibe—so intrigued Cole it addled his brain to the point of this crazy compromise.

Suddenly the quiet month of June he always looked forward to, vacationing in his family summer home on the Gulf, was to be shared by a quarrelsome little Puritan with sultry lips and wide-set, bedroom eyes that spoke bewitching volumes, but not a syllable they spoke was a conscious come-on.

Muttering a curse, he turned away and grabbed up his paintbrush, furious with himself for caving in. This was *his* month, blast it! He'd looked forward to this vacation as a balm to help ease his grief over the recent death of his father. Not to mention his need for an escape from business stress, which up to yesterday had been brutal, battling a hostile takeover bid for the largest of his holdings, Quad-State Oil and Gas. The pressure had been incessant and deadly. The poison pill he devised to hold on to the company had been a successful tactic, making the purchase unpalatably expensive for the challenger. He was weary from eighteen-hour days, mentally and emotionally drained. He needed the escape he found here to do nothing but relax, listen to the surf or take on some welcome, physical exertion.

He loved this house and the childhood memories it brought with it, of happy times with his doting father. The man who, at fifty-five years of age, took in a newborn child, gave him a name, raised him, nurtured him and passed on his wisdom. Seeing to the property's upkeep restored Cole, made him happy. Because of his care, year by year, he kept the beloved place whole and beautiful.

Working with his hands in solitude by the sea, Cole could quietly reflect, spend time getting reacquainted with his imagination. Through unaccompanied toil and thought, he connected with men of bygone ages who helped steer his hands. These reclusive vacations exercised his mind and his soul as well as his body. Each year he looked forward to June, to this place, coming away from it energized, revived, ready for the rat race again.

He began to brush white paint on the fence, his failure to handle the intrusion as he'd planned affecting him in deep, disturbing ways. What was his problem? What was it about this female that had the power to short circuit his intentions?

"Maybe we should—exchange names?"

He shot her a perturbed look and she stared at him. Her annoyance was so evident from her pinkened cheeks and sparking eyes, he experienced a surprise prickle of appreciation. *Damn,* she was stubborn. He wondered what her meetings were all about. What her applicants might apply for. Nothing kinky, he suspected. She was too prim and punctilious to be up to any pornographic shenanigans.

"Call me Cole," he muttered. "Cole—Noone." Though he was "Cole" to his friends, he smirked inwardly at the hurriedly conjured last name. Noone—shoving together the words "no" and "one." She thought he was a handyman. He'd let her. It might be interesting to observe how a woman reacted to him when she *didn't* know he was J. C. Barringer, wealthy capitalist. Ordinarily women fawned over him, cooing, petting and fluttering lashes. So far, from this female, he hadn't detected a single coo or flutter.

She surprised him by sticking out a hand, apparently expecting him to take it. "I'm Jennifer Sancroft."

Something about that name nudged his memory. Jennifer Sancroft. Why did that name seem familiar? He closed his eyes for a moment, too tired and annoyed to worry about it. It would come to him. Since she was renting the corporate property, she had to work for one of his companies, or one of his father's that he'd just taken over. He'd no doubt heard it in a business reference.

For some unfathomable reason—possibly the insidious influence of those sensual lips—he took her hand in his. Her skin was cool, as he'd expected, her handshake firm. "How do you do, Miss Sancroft," he said, his tone wholly unwelcoming.

"How do you know it's Miss?" she asked, her features quizzical.

He couldn't contain the amused twitch of his lips. Was she kidding? "Just a guess."

Her cheeks flushed. She'd caught his sarcasm. Tugging her fingers from his, she lifted her shoulders. Any more attempts to be intimidatingly tall and her sensible brown pumps would lift off the ground. "Well..." She backed up another step. "I'll go get unpacked." She pivoted away, retreating across the lawn.

He watched her go, aggravation twisting his gut. Now that he could no longer be affected by those cupid's-bow lips and unconsciously sexy eyes, he willed her to walk to the car, slide in and disappear.

When she reached her vehicle, she popped the trunk and pulled out a suitcase. Cole gritted out an oath. So much for his telepathic powers.

Ruthie flung open the front door as her boss approached. "So, is he leaving on Sunday?" Her expression more worried than hopeful, she hurried off the covered porch and grabbed one of the bags. Married or not, the look on Ruthie's face made it clear she'd be happy to have Mr. Eye-Candy hang around for the whole three weeks.

Jen heaved a sigh, mounting the two steps to the columned colonial porch. "He's not leaving." Once inside, she set down her suitcase and looked around absently. "He seemed—reluctant—to change his plans. I said he could stay." The ugly truth, that "reluctant" was a mild description of his attitude, remained Jen's secret. Her assistant didn't need to know she hadn't graciously allowed the handyman to stay on out of the goodness of her heart.

"Excellent!" Ruthie's expression brightened. "We need a good view around here."

"The Gulf of Mexico is practically in the backyard."

Ruthie waved that off as insignificant. "No offense, boss, but you'd think considering why you're here, you'd be more interested in looking at men."

Jen ignored her assistant's gibe. "Yes, well—this is more of a partnership than a—a—physical attraction match." She didn't like Ruthie's doubtful expression. "There's no logical reason why I can't find a perfectly respectable husband this way. Compatibility and common interests are very important. Why, my own parents—"

"I know, boss," Ruthie cut in, her tone pensive, almost pitying. "Your parents are a great team—with mutual goals. A great example of a sensible union."

"Don't forget, I know all about the treacherousness of blind devotion," she said, a knee-jerk defense.

Ruthie nodded, looking sad. "Tony." Her rueful gaze met her boss's. "I know. Remember, I was your assistant when he broke your heart. But I think it's wrong to give up on love because of one jerk."

"I'm not giving up on love." Jen was weary of trying to get Ruthie to understand.

"Sure, boss," Ruthie mumbled. "You think love can grow if two compatible people work at it." She couldn't make it plainer she wasn't one hundred percent on board with Jen's theory.

Refusing to defend her rationale again, Jen clamped her jaws. She'd made it abundantly clear why she'd decided to find a husband in such an unorthodox way.

Jen felt fortunate her assistant was accustomed to keeping her own counsel and wouldn't gossip about Jen's socalled "vacation." Everybody else at the accounting firm thought Jen was getting quietly married and on her honeymoon. All but Ruthie. Looking at her dubious expression, if there had been any way Jen could have handled this husband hunt alone, she would have.

"Well, at least the place is nice." Ruthie's remark drew Jen from her mental wanderings. Indicating a staircase at the end of the wide entry, her assistant went on. "That leads up to the bedrooms. Naturally, you'll want the master. There's a guest room right across the head of the stairs for me."

Jen cast a glance at the staircase. A landing, halfway up, caught her eye. A tall window in the back wall revealed a cloudless sky. "Mm-hmm. Bedroom," she mumbled.

"I figured we could set up interviews at the dining table here." Ruthie indicated the formal dining room to the left of the entry. A carved oak china cabinet dominated the wall behind a glass-topped table. Jen noted the table's base looked like four columns set into a central pedestal. The massive base had been created from some kind of light-colored stone. The table wasn't huge, but it looked to be about six feet square. Two elegant chairs made of light wood stood on each of the four sides.

"Unless you'd rather interview over there." Ruthie indicated a location behind Jen and she turned to view the sprawling living room. A fireplace with a white, marble surround dominated the far end. Though situated on the north of the house, three tall windows let in plenty of light.

Decor in pale pastels helped keep the room airy and light. Sheer window treatments swagged and swooped and puddled attractively. While not so sheer as to prevent a degree of privacy, they allowed in diffused sunlight. Strategically located in massive ceramic pots, scatterings of green foliage enlivened the space. The pale hues and muted radiance of the room reminded Jen of a certain pair of eyes.

"Pretty," Ruthie murmured, coming up beside her boss.

"Yes, he is."

"Huh?" Ruthie's skeptical query yanked Jen from her musings. "I was talking about the house, not the hunk."

Jen had a bad feeling she'd said something she hadn't

meant to say—and would deny to her dying day. "So was I—talking about the house!" She made sure neither her tone nor her expression allowed room for argument. She had enough to deal with without entering into a debate over whether she suffered from some daft fixation for a certain arrogant handyman.

CHAPTER TWO

COLE couldn't help noticing the prissy little gate-crasher kept her distance for the remainder of the weekend. The other one, the freckled one with the barking laugh, was more sociable. She waved greetings whenever their paths happened to cross. The frosty one, the one he'd dubbed Miss Priss, stayed inside. That was too bad. Not that he had any desire to see her. It wasn't that. It was just that she was pale. Walking on the beach, catching a few rays, would do her some good.

Monday morning, as he headed out of the surf after an energizing swim, he noticed a strange car in the drive. Toweling his hair, he wondered what kind of interviews these two women were holding. He shrugged it off. What in blazes did he care? He had things to do.

Even though Cole worked hard on his disinterest, he couldn't help noticing that every half hour a car pulled into the drive as the previous one drove away. Around two in the afternoon, he decided to trim dead limbs high in a live oak near the front of the house.

From up there he had an excellent view of the driveway. The sound of tires crunching over gravel caught his attention as one car drove off and another arrived. A thin, balding man in a chocolate-brown suit stepped out of the ebony compact. It occurred to Cole that not once today had he seen a woman arrive. All visitors had been men in three-piece suits. Most carried briefcases.

Cole had a healthy curiosity, but he wasn't nosy. Nevertheless, every time a car pulled up and another man got out, he couldn't help but wonder what was going on inside the residence.

At four, he finished the tree trimming and climbed down. Aggravated with himself for this weird preoccupation with the goings-on in the main house, he grabbed up his toolbox. He had to know what those females were up to. Miss Priss had made it plain she didn't want him banging around inside the house. But the leaky kitchen faucet required nothing noisy, only a washer. He could do that very quietly.

He headed around the rear of the house and bounded up the eight wooden steps to the expansive, covered deck. With as little noise as possible, he slipped inside the back door that led into a rustic den and open kitchen. This was his favorite place in the big house. Less formal than the front rooms, its leather furniture and American-Indian decor was more to his taste. Instead of carpeting, the floor consisted of wide oak planking. The fireplace was constructed of stone instead of marble. Though he enjoyed staying in the cottage on these solitary visits, preferring its rustic intimacy, the big house brought back fond memories.

He ambled around the green- and gold-flecked granite eating bar separating the kitchen from the den, and set his toolbox on the stone countertop. Metal against granite clanked and he grimaced. So much for being quiet. He heard shuffling and turned. Little Ms. Freckle-face peered around the door frame from the entry hallway. Her concerned expression opened in a grin, and she whispered, "Oh, I thought you were a burglar."

He gave her a skeptical once-over. "What would you have done if I were?"

"Kicked you to heck-and-gone, handsome." She entered the kitchen and leaned against the counter nearest the doorway. "I was a sergeant in the Marines. Covert Ops. If I wanted to I could drop you where you stand."

He grinned. "Are you flirting with me?"

Laughing, she held up her left hand to show him her wedding set. "No—but it crossed my mind."

"Ruthie?" Miss Priss called from the living room. "The next candidate just drove up."

"So your name's Ruthie?" Cole kept his voice low enough so he couldn't be heard outside the kitchen.

"Ruthie Tuttle." She headed toward him, hand outstretched. "And the boss tells me you're Cole Noone," she whispered. "Nice to officially meet you, Noone."

He took her hand and leaned closer to murmur, "I think it's best if you don't mention I'm here."

She winked conspiratorially. "Gotcha. The boss'd have my head if she knew. She's got enough to do without beheading me. Besides, I really, *really* want that dripping to stop. The last two nights it drove me bonkers."

"You could hear it all the way upstairs?"

Her grin wrinkled her nose. "I have the ears of a bat."

The doorbell chimed. "Ruthie! What are you doing in there? Please, get the door."

The redheaded assistant made a face, mouthing, "Duty calls." She hurried around the corner. "On my way, boss."

Cole turned to his work. During the next fifteen minutes, he slowly, soundlessly replaced the washer, his attention focused more on the interview in the living room than on the repair job. He couldn't make out every word, but what he did hear he found difficult to believe.

It sounded as though Miss Sancroft was interviewing for a husband. Finished with the repair, he laid the flats of his hands on the cool granite and shook his head, strangely disappointed. He wasn't surprised by much, but *that* surprised him. He had a hard time restraining his irritation. Why in the name of all that was nuts in the world, would she resort to such a stupid, *sterile* plan? With eyes like hers? And those lips! Surely some of the men she'd dated would have looked past her drab, frumpish clothes and seen—

"Well—thank you for your time, Mr. Robertson."

Cole glanced over his shoulder. Miss Sultry-lips sounded closer.

"It was—interesting," the man said with a tense laugh. "Goodbye, Ms. Sancroft. Good luck."

"Thank you for coming."

Cole heard the door close, then silence.

"When's the next appointment, Ruthie?"

"Not for fifteen or twenty minutes. He called to say his flight had been delayed."

"Thank heaven." Cole heard her sigh. "I need a break. I think I'll have a health nut bar and a cup of instant—" She rounded the corner into the kitchen. Her sentence and her forward movement ended when she saw him. Outrage transformed her features. *"You!"*

He shifted to fully face her and lounged against the counter. Crossing his arms over his bare chest, he eyed her critically. She wore a white blouse with long sleeves and a high, Puritan neckline. Her shapeless, gray skirt hit her midknee. Between the skirt hem and her sensible pumps, he saw slender, attractive legs that could be shown off to better advantage.

She wore her hair slicked back the same, sexless way she'd worn it on Saturday. Even so, the extremely unattractive style couldn't quite make her plain. Her vivid, jade eyes, full lips and great bone structure were difficult to spoil, no matter how hard she might try. He wondered why she was trying so hard.

The stillness crackled with tension. Cole was unaccustomed to being glared at by women. He ignored the prickle of irritation and eyed her without smiling. "Afternoon."

His chilly greeting seemed to revive her from her paralysis and she threw him a stiff-armed point. *"You* are not supposed to be in here."

Another thing Cole was unaccustomed to was being told he wasn't supposed to be somewhere. His irritation billowed, but he didn't let it show. "I didn't make noise."

She gasped. "You—*that's not the point!* You were *not* supposed to come inside during my interviews! I specifically ordered you not to!"

He stared for a count of ten. During the stretched-out silence she exhaled with agitation, plainly upset by his dawdling to get on with his groveling and apologizing. Well, she'd have a long wait.

"I don't take orders well," he said, then turned away, dismissing her with body language. Hefting his toolbox he strode around the eating bar toward the rear door. With his hand on the knob, he halted and glanced back. "Why in Hades are you interviewing for a husband?"

Her mouth dropped open at his bluntness. "Get out!" she demanded, her voice as rusty as an old tin can.

Jen felt shell-shocked. After nearly three days holed up inside that house, she needed to get out, walk off her frustrations. Even if it meant chancing a run-in with the insolent handyman. Why should she hide? She was the sanctioned occupant here, legally leasing this place. She had a right to enjoy the beach. After the horrendous day she'd had, if she didn't do something besides stare at the walls, she would scream. She was customarily optimistic and confident, but today both her optimism and her confidence had been sorely tested.

She vaulted off the sofa where she'd held so many unproductive interviews. "I'm going for a walk, Ruthie."

Her secretary sat on a wing chair placed at an angle to the couch. She looked up, flipped her notepad closed and nodded. "It's about time you got out and enjoyed the nice weather." She stood. "I'm going upstairs to call Raymond, see how he and the kids are dealing with his parents' visit." She rolled her eyes. "I can hardly stand the suspense."

"Fine," Jen murmured, too preoccupied with today's futile interviews to say more. She was out of the living room and almost to the kitchen before Ruthie called after her.

"Boss?"

Jen glanced back. "Yes?"

"Should I order take-out for dinner?"

Jen shrugged, not feeling much like eating. "Sure."

"For about an hour from now?"

"Sure." She glanced at her watch. Five-thirty. She had

plenty of time to walk off her anxieties. Well, at least she had *some* time. She didn't think all the time in the world, or all the strength she could muster, would allow her to walk off all her troubles.

She went out the back door and stood for a moment on the wood deck. Wicker furniture with red-and-blue-striped cushions brightened the shady area. Potted gardenia plants, with glossy green leaves and a multitude of white blossoms, lent delicate beauty to the space, their breeze-tossed, flowery fragrance mingling agreeably with the briny tang of the Gulf.

The rustling of a wind through the sea grasses on the dunes beyond the freshly painted pickets, the rush of the surf, eased her stress slightly. How miraculous that only a moment in the relaxing magic of nature's grandeur could have an effect.

She inhaled, deciding this walk on the beach was days overdue. Provoking handyman or not, she needed this, needed the gentle relief of sun and surf to ease the coil of anxiety that had taken up residence inside her.

She walked down the steps to the lawn, focusing determinedly on the beach. She strode to the fence, unlatched the gate and headed over the dunes to tawny sand. She came to a stop just out of reach of the skittering surf. The high-pitched cry of a seagull swooping nearby attracted her attention. She watched the bird dip and soar over the boundless Gulf. The view was gorgeous, with the brilliance of a late-afternoon sun glinting off the azure blue. It was so quiet, so restful, she could feel the pressures of the distressing day melt away.

Edgy, worrisome thoughts tried to intrude—of the reason she had to be there, of all that depended on these next weeks. She tried not to let her anger and frustration over the unfairness of the world come to the surface. She'd spent too much time lately letting it get to her.

Here she was, on a pristine beach, breathing in fresh, sea air, her face caressed by sunshine. She shouldn't contaminate the moment by dwelling on her troubles. Through exhaustively long work days and total devotion to her career, she'd becoming the youngest, and only female, of three vice presidents. Then last week, when the current president abruptly announced he was leaving for a job out of state, Jen knew, by any fair measurement, she *deserved* the presidency.

It was her tough luck that the owner and absentee CEO of the firm had ruled with raging conservatism over the years, never promoting a bachelor to the presidency—let alone a female—always opting for a settled, family man. Though the elderly owner recently passed away, and control passed to his son, Jen feared the governing beliefs of the heir would be equally unprogressive. What did it matter to this newest owner that the firm had become a substitute for a family? The fact that she was a thirty-one-year-old woman and single should *not* matter! Unfortunately, at the heart of the accounting business was a hard knot of conservatism that couldn't be unraveled. Inflexible, old-guard thinking made her crazy.

The new CEO, equally reclusive and all-powerful, had sent a gold-embossed missive to each of the three vice presidents that he would interview the candidates within the next three weeks. Jen's discovery that her interview would be last was like a slap in the face. She took it as a bleak sign, since as Tax Vice President, she had what was considered the most prestigious post. Suddenly, and with stark clarity, she had seen the handwriting on the wall.

Maybe she had gone a little crazy. Maybe it was partly because over the past year or so her biological clock's ticking had grown loud in her head. What had begun as a faint whisper, had grown steadily, bringing with it flutterings of a desire for more in life than business success, a craving for her own two-point-four children.

She wanted a career and she wanted a family. As president she could have both. Her plans included working-mother-friendly programs, like on-site day care and job sharing for support staff who would like to work half days so they could spend more time at home with children. Jen also planned to initiate eight weeks of paid maternity leave. In addition, mothers would be allowed to keep newborns in the office, and a lactation and child care consultant would be hired.

D.A.A. was woefully behind the times when it came to its married female employees and their needs. The company, too, could use updating in other ways, and Jen had plans there, too. She had no doubt she could transform the small, prestigious firm into one of the most respected in Texas.

She hadn't planned to find a husband quite this quickly, or precisely this way, but to have a shot at the presidency she must be stable and settled. The presidential-quality Jennifer Sancroft *must* arrive at that interview with a legitimate, accomplished spouse.

She'd had no choice but to act and act now. In her unwavering, intense way, the plan to correct her marital status had been hatched and put into action. With a mere eighteen days until the fateful audience with the company's CEO, she had to focus like she'd never focused before. She *must* have a supportive spouse, *must* be settled and family oriented.

By heaven, she would succeed!

Jen stretched then lowered her arms, exhaling. She raised her arms again, taking in a deep breath, working to restore her confidence. "Don't worry, Jen," she told herself. "Tomorrow will be better. They won't all be as discouraging as they were today. So what if a few of them looked at you like you're insane?"

Maybe she should have put the word "marriage" in her *Wall Street Journal* advertisement. The closest she'd come to even hinting at matrimony had been a few phrases like, "successful businessman, tired of the rat race, looking for new challenges," sprinkled among more sterile requirements like "excellent people skills," "degree required" and "loyalty a plus."

What had she thought would happen, that Mr. Right would sweep in, take one look at her and fall to his knees begging her to marry him? "Ha!" she scoffed. "Way to go, Jen. Your optimism certainly isn't hindered by sound reasoning!"

She hadn't been able to bring herself to place a personal ad. It seemed too lurid for her high-minded intention. The truth was, her pride hadn't allowed her to solicit a mate in a personal ad. Considering her restrained, conservative upbringing, a businesslike request through the *Wall Street Journal* held the right note of respectability and civility.

Besides, her mind whispered, *keeping your search on a business plane reduced the taint of desperation.*

She winced, muttering, "Unfortunately, your precious business plane didn't have the directness that would have cut down on the looks of horror on a few faces."

A handful of the men looked at her like she was from another planet. The memory stung. Deflated, she dropped her arms to her side. Today's interviews were too depressing to dwell on. "How dare they be insulted!" she muttered.

She felt something wet and looked down to see the surf skittering across her shoes and sloshing inside. "Oh, fine!" She hopped back, too late. Pulling off one pump then the other, she dumped out seawater. "That's just great!"

"What do you expect, coming out here wearing those?" came a voice from behind her.

Jolted by the nearness of the male voice, Jen jumped, almost stumbled. She made a pained face, willing him to disappear.

"Why don't you take off your stockings, Miss Sancroft? Beach sand is meant to seep between your toes."

Trying to appear unruffled, she didn't respond or turn around, but went about shaking the last of the water from her suede shoes.

"Here." He nudged her arm.

She didn't want to acknowledge him, but he was making it tough. Annoyed that she couldn't seem to stop herself, she peered in his direction. To her astonishment, he held out a glass of iced tea. A sprig of fresh mint sprouted festively from the tumbler. She eyed the glass suspiciously, then transferred her stare to his face. "What's this?"

His lips twitched as though he found her question ludicrous. "Take a wild guess."

She faced him, holding up her pumps, one in each fist. "I don't have any place to put it."

He examined her shoe-filled hands. Without a word he snatched first one shoe then the other, tossing them over his shoulder. She gasped as they sailed above the fence and landed on the lawn. "There." He held out the tea. "Now you do."

She glowered at him. "You—you *threw* my shoes!"

His laugh was deep and rich even with its derisive edge, causing a tingle to dance along her spine. She squelched the tickle with a shoulder-squaring stance.

"Take the tea, Miss Sancroft." He indicated her with a nod. "You have to be sweltering in all those clothes."

She couldn't believe his audacity. "I don't care for any tea," she said. "And I'm not a bit hot."

His lips twitched again, as though he were laughing at her. "I won't argue that."

She eyed him dubiously. Had he deferred to her or insulted her?

He lifted the glass as though in a toast, and took a sip. "Your loss. I make great tea."

She didn't like to admit it, but she was hot and uncomfortable and she was ruining a perfectly good pair of stockings. With a harrumph, she turned away. Grateful her skirt was full, she inched it up until she could reach the elasticized rim of her thigh-high stocking and began to roll the nylon down her leg.

"What are you doing?" he asked.

"Go away."

"Ah—taking off your stockings."

She cast him a grim look. "I hope you're enjoying the show!"

He'd cocked his head to better check out her stocking striptease. When their gazes clashed, he lifted his glass in her direction, as though in a toast to her bare leg. Heat flamed in her cheeks and she flipped her skirt down to cover her thigh.

He indicated her with the tumbler. "I feel like I owe you a sip now."

"I'm not taking off my stockings for your gratification, Mr. Noone!" She turned her back, easing the stocking off her foot. Her balance wasn't good in the damp sand, but she managed it. Not knowing what else to do with the nylon, she draped it across her shoulder and eased up her skirt on the other side to get the second stocking off.

"There ought to be music for this."

She ignored him, but her face flamed. It wasn't all due to the fact that she was overdressed for standing on a Texas beach in June. She finally got the other stocking off and tossed it across her shoulder with its mate. Straightening, she unbuttoned a cuff and rolled her sleeve up to her elbow, then did the same with the other.

She hadn't heard any lewd comments for a full half minute, so she had high hopes he'd gone away as quietly as he'd arrived. She peered around to check and was unsettled to find that he'd taken a seat on the sand, crossed his legs at the ankles and was watching her. "Don't stop now," he said.

She faced him, irked. She would not let herself be flustered by this guy! She disciplined her voice. "I hadn't planned to stop." She unbuttoned the top two—no three—buttons of her blouse.

His eyes swept over her speculatively. "Go on."

She wiped a hand across her forehead to banish telltale beads of sweat. "That's the end of the show."

"What a shame," he said, his mocking evident. He held up the half-empty glass. "Thirsty, yet?"

Refusing to admit she was, she shook her head. "I'm going for a walk."

He nodded. "Good idea." He indicated the incoming tide. "Walk in the surf, it'll cool you down."

She made a guttural sound of aggravation. "I'm from Dallas, I know all the ins and outs of walking on Gulf of Mexico beaches."

"Right." He glanced pointedly at the stockings riding her shoulder. "Just to update you, some people take off their stockings *before* they hit the sand."

She blew out a puff of air, aiming the draft at her bodice, hoping some of it would slip beneath the fabric and cool her sweltering skin. "It's a free country," she said. "You have a right to pass along unwanted advice."

She spun away and headed toward the undulating surf. He was right, of course. The water rushing around her ankles would make her cooler. She sloshed into the tide. Oh, how refreshing it felt. And the squishy sand between her toes was delicious. If she'd been alone, she might even have allowed herself a smile.

"You didn't say why you were interviewing for a husband," he said, sounding like he'd stood up and was trailing her. "Pregnant?"

Unsettled by his nearness and his choice of subjects, she aimed a dagger-filled glare his way. "Do *not* follow me and *no,* of course I'm not pregnant!"

"I didn't think so." He caught up with her. "Okay, I admit you might not be the sexiest thing on two legs, but you're no dog. Why advertise?"

She stopped and glared at him. "Are you horribly insensitive or just horribly dense?"

He halted beside her. Taking a sip of the tea, he considered her over the rim of the glass. The eye contact seemed to go on forever and Jen began to detect an odd, disconcerting buzzing in her head—as though brain wires were shorting out. His eyes had a debilitating effect but she continued to endure the contact. If he thought she was going to justify herself to him, he was very wrong.

He lowered the glass to the accompaniment of clinking ice, and drawled coolly, "Just curious."

Her anger flared. "Look, you have a job to do, so do it and stay out of my personal life."

His dark hair ruffled as saucy Madam Sea Breeze ran flirtatious fingers through it. He watched her for a few seconds, his expression hard. "If an employee of mine did something as idiotic as advertising for a husband," he said, "I'd fire her." He continued his direct inspection until she was so uneasy she had to turn away.

How dare he have the gall to speak to her that way. Her focus shifted and skidded over the water, up to the clear sky as inwardly she bridled at her rare bout of uncertainty. Regaining her conviction she scowled at him, so angry she could hardly breathe. "Well, Mr. Noone," she said, "since the way I find a husband isn't my employer's business, it's fortunate for you—because of the lawsuit I'd slap you with—that I *don't* work for you!"

Cole watched her stalk off through the surf, the irony of her frosty threat chilling the air around him. Since his beach house was only available to employees of the companies he owned, at some level or other, Miss Priss *did* work for him. Not directly, of course, but somewhere in the pecking order of one of his firms. He rubbed his eyes. She was right about the lawsuit. How she got a husband wasn't his business, as long as she did her job. His personal prejudices shouldn't enter into his business dealings.

He wasn't about to tell her she really did work for him. Not yet, anyway. She confounded him, intrigued him and annoyed him. She had no idea he was anything other than a handyman. For that reason alone she was worth scrutinizing—to see how a woman who was oblivious to his wealth and power reacted to him. So far his little experiment hadn't done his ego much good.

Mainly, his curiosity was driving him nuts. He had to know why she would resort to a bizarre plan to acquire a husband the way most people would buy a used TV. The outcome of her project, not to mention discovering her reasons for it, drew him even though the very idea infuriated the fire out of him. He wasn't sure when—if ever—any one woman had brought out so many conflicting emotions in him all at one time.

His resentment gaining intensity, he mumbled, "Stubborn little idiot." He shook his head, staring after her. "How did women get the reputation for being the romantic sex?"

Cole knew plenty of females who didn't take love into consideration when picking a mate. Over the years, he'd had his share of clinging opportunists with varying self-serving motives. Money, position, power, prestige and celebrity were just a few.

But what was Miss Priss's motive? What did she have against falling in love?

Cole knew how powerful an emotion love could be. Albert Barringer, his father, never got over his love for Adrianne Bourne, a twenty-year-old high-fashion model he'd had a brief affair with. The elder entrepreneur was wise enough to understand that the young beauty was using him to gain access to his wealth and position. But Albert had been in love, so he simply reveled in her affection for as long as she offered it, keeping his foreboding of her looming abandonment locked in his heart.

Not once over the years after Adrianne dumped him had Albert spoken negatively of her. Even though she readily, even eagerly, gave up all rights to their newborn son in exchange for Albert's Hollywood contacts.

All these years, knowing his own mother bartered him away—for stardom—had been a difficult truth for Cole to live with. His father's unwavering devotion to his only son made up for a lot. He'd taught Cole well in the ways of business. Yet he also taught him something else, something unspoken and tragically sad, that abided forever in his father's eyes—how all-consuming and tragic love could be.

Long ago Cole vowed never to lose his heart unless it was real for *both* him and that one, special woman. He would *not* end up like his father, with only distant, tattered memories of love lost.

He flicked his glance to the woman on the beach. She stooped to pick up a seashell, straightened brushing sand from her prize. "Love is a dangerous thing to trifle with, Miss Sancroft," he murmured. "What in Hades are you scheming?"

CHAPTER THREE

COLE had lots of time to reflect on the frustrating and fascinating Miss Sancroft as he cut and stacked limbs he'd pruned from the live oak the day before. The metal rack where he piled the wood was around the back of the house. Even so, he could hear cars come and go all day. Every time another set of tires crunched over the gravel and pulled to a stop in front of the beach house, his anger heightened a notch.

Old memories of his youth, sneaking off to the movies to see his mother on the huge screen, smiling, faking sweet vulnerability, added fuel to the fire. Adrianne Bourne, the queen of grasping females, had become the Hollywood star she'd schemed and clawed to be. Now, in her mid-fifties, she was still a beauty and occasionally played character roles. Married to her fifth boy-toy, she may have been a beloved Hollywood icon, but to Cole, his mother was a cold-hearted, calculating woman who'd never once contacted her only son.

By the time six o'clock rolled around, Cole was hot, tired and thoroughly incensed—mainly at himself—for letting the woman interviewing for husbands in his beach house get under his skin. Let her do whatever she wanted. What was it to him?

Even after counseling with himself, when she came out of the back door onto the deck to gaze out to sea, he stopped work, leaned against the warm brick wall and observed her over the woodpile. He scanned her as she walked to a chair and sat down. To his surprise, she removed her leather shoes, setting them aside. Then she slid her hands up one leg and began to slip off a stocking.

The unobstructed glimpse of pale thigh startled him. Apparently she was so preoccupied with her thoughts she didn't even consider someone might be nearby. After slipping the stocking off, she carefully folded it. After placing it in a shoe she went about removing the other stocking. As she did, her navy skirt remained high on her legs. Nice legs. He'd observed that on the beach when she'd been much more self-conscious about taking the garments off. He felt like he should make himself known, or turn away, but he did neither.

She deposited the second stocking neatly in the other shoe. Standing, she straightened her skirt and gazed out to sea. In the shapeless navy skirt and mannish, short-sleeve Oxford-cloth shirt, she looked like a repressed schoolmarm, even barefoot.

After another moment of silently staring, she turned in his direction and padded to the steps that led to the lawn. Her features were pensive, her forehead creased in what looked like unhappy thoughts. Unfortunately for Cole, her solemn expression didn't diminish the effect her pouty lips had on him—siren-like in their sensuality—consuming his attention. Even with her hair swept back in that unbecoming style she was beautiful. A truth he didn't enjoy admitting.

As she walked down the steps, he stepped into view. Lifting a log, he purposely dropped it on the stack to make noise. She started, green eyes shooting in his direction.

"Evening." He nodded without smiling.

"Have you been there all along!" she asked.

He stripped off his work gloves and tossed them onto the rick of wood. "I wasn't born here, but I've been here most of the day."

Her features grew pinched. "You could have made yourself known!"

He allowed himself a scornful smile. "If you're talking about the stocking strip show, honey, I've seen lewder sights at G-rated movies."

"Maybe you should keep your eyes on the screen!"

He laughed. She had a quick wit; he had to give her that. "Bad day?" he asked.

She blinked, shifting her attention to the Gulf. "*Perfect* day." Stepping onto the grass, she pivoting toward the water. "Goodbye."

He almost smiled at her brush-off. Did she really think it would be that easy? He cleared his throat and followed after her. "Perfect? I gather you've found a number of hot prospects in your husband hunt?" He caught up with her as she reached the gate. Releasing the latch, he motioned for her to precede him.

With her nose in the air and a muttered "Thank you" on her lips, she did. She'd scurried five feet away by the time he secured the gate. Broadening his pace, he reached her side in a half dozen strides. "You don't say? That many?" He slid his hands into his back pockets, keeping his demeanor more carelessly curious than rankled.

She gave him a dark look but didn't take the bait.

He pressed on. "Tell me again why you're interviewing for husbands?" he prodded. "It slipped my mind."

Though he could tell she detested the need to, she returned her gaze to his, making it clear from her expression she was not amused by his pestering. "Look, I just want to walk on my beach. It *is* mine. I'm paying for the right to use it."

Her cutting glare could have drawn blood from a lesser man. Even Cole felt its jab. She turned away and hurried off. "Oh, right," he drawled, deciding to theorize why she was there. Clearly she had no intention of telling him without some manipulation. "It's that career move, right?"

She faltered but recovered quickly, whirling to confront him. "I didn't tell you about the promotion. Did Ruthie?"

Damnation. Why did he have to be right? He would have given a lot not to be. Hiding his anger behind a mask of indifference, he walked up to join her. "Ruthie didn't say a word." When they were toe to toe, he dropped the bomb. "You did. Just now."

She inhaled sharply; her cheeks going pink. "That was a dirty trick."

He shook his head. "No dirtier than the one you're going to play on some unsuspecting man."

Her eyes went wide. "What are you talking about?"

He could no longer hide his anger. Towering over her, he leaned forward, fixing his eyes on her like gun barrels. "I'm talking about the poor guy you marry. What happens when you're through using him? Does hubby get severance pay?" Without giving her a chance to reply, he went on. "What job could be so all-fired important that you'd make this mad dash to snag a husband? What kind of work even has *husband* in its job requirements?"

She took a step backward, clearly intimidated by his animosity and his height. Even so she matched his stance, defiantly jutting her chin. "The job is none of your business, but just to be clear, the man I choose to marry I'll marry for *keeps!*"

He couldn't believe such ludicrous tripe and responded with a hollow laugh. "Yeah, sure—and the check is in the mail."

"Are you calling me a liar?"

His laugh died and so did his smile. "If you're not lying, you're deluded."

"You have some nerve!" She kneaded her temples as though trying to ward off a headache. "You don't know me! You don't have any right to presume anything about me!"

"I know plenty of women like you."

Her lips sagged and she made a low, guttural sound. He tensed for the attack he knew was coming. She lashed out with a hand, but he caught her before she made contact with his face. Her arm trapped in his fist, she bared her teeth. "I don't know what kind of women you know, and

I swear I don't want to know.'' She jerked on his grasp. ''Let *go!*''

''So you can take another shot at me? Do you think I'm stupid?''

She yanked on his hold, glared at him, but didn't reply. She didn't have to. *Of course, I think you're stupid,* glittered in her eyes.

With a muttered oath, he released her.

Surprised, she stumbled several steps.

''Maybe you shouldn't bad-mouth stupidity, honey,'' he muttered. ''Only a guy with nothing going on between the ears would agree to some half-baked marriage scheme.''

''Then you'd be perfect for the job!'' she cried, her eyes a blink away from tears.

''So where do I get in line?'' That crazy question came out of nowhere. The shock on her face was no more staggering than the shock he felt from hearing the inquiry in his own voice.

She closed her mouth, swallowed, then whispered hoarsely, ''What?''

He shoved a hand through his hair and counted to ten to restore his composure. He told himself he was being sarcastic—to shake her up. He'd succeeded, he could tell. With a crooked smile that felt tight, he said, ''In your opinion, I'm stupid enough to be perfect. So—where's the line?''

Her expression mutated from a stunned stare to a murderous glare. ''Don't be ridiculous,'' she said. ''My husband would need credentials. At least a college degree— advanced would be better.'' She licked her lips, obviously grasping at any straw that would convince this lowly handyman he didn't have a chance at marrying her, no matter how desperate she might become. ''And—and...'' she went on, ''he must be able to converse with intelligent, educated businessmen who have money, position and power.''

He eyed heaven theatrically, deciding words weren't necessary to convey his contempt.

"I don't care what you think. There are logical, level-headed men out there who can understand that two intelligent people with the right attitude and similar goals can make a good marriage!"

"Bull."

Their eyes traded stinging hostilities before she responded. "I couldn't expect *you* to comprehend. I imagine you'd be hard pressed to understand anything more complicated than peeling bananas with your toes and—and swinging around in trees!"

"Are you calling me an ape?"

She winced and he sensed she wasn't in the habit of insulting people. "Forget it." She turned away to stare out to sea. "I just want to be left alone. Even a not-so-bright *ape* could see that."

He felt an unexpected twinge of compassion but shook it off. She was planning to use some poor jerk to advance her career. She didn't deserve compassion. "For the record," he asked, "how many logical, advanced-degreed Nobel prize winners have loved your proposition so far?"

She bit her lip, her only reaction.

"That many?"

She cast him a furtive glance. "I have very high standards."

From her pensive preoccupation earlier, he bet much of the turning down hadn't been on her part. Deciding she needed taking down a peg he meandered casually around her, making it clear he was checking her out from all angles. "Mm-hmm," he said when he'd finished his leisurely circuit.

She glared at him. "What is that supposed to mean!"

"It means, men have standards, too, Miss Sancroft."

A glint of uneasiness in her eyes told him he'd hit a nerve. "What—what are you saying?"

With the flick of his hand he indicated her attire. "Look at you." He pursed his lips and shook his head. "I may not have the most aristocratic résumé as potential husbands go, but I know what men want." He allowed a stony silence to lengthen between them before he let her have it right between the eyes. "And it's not a priggish, cold-fish virgin."

"Priggish?" Shock edged her tone. "Cold fish? How dare you!" He noticed she stopped short of repeating "virgin" and thought that significant. It was like admitting that part, at least, she couldn't dispute. "You don't know what you're talking about!" She spun away and stalked off.

"Like hell I don't!" He followed, grasping her arm. "When you need expert advice, Miss Sancroft, you'd be wise to listen to an expert."

She jerked to face him. "And you're an expert on women?"

His knowing smile was his answer.

She yanked on his hold. "Well, I'm not trying to attract your type!"

"Honey, when it comes to what men want in a woman, I'm the only type." He let her go and reached around behind her head, slipping several pins from her hair. The stuff began to unwrap from its tight coil.

"What do you think—"

"Shut up and pay attention." He tugged the hair gently until it came loose and cascaded down her back. "Shake it out."

She stared at him as though he was speaking some bizarre foreign tongue.

When it became obvious she wasn't computing his command, he gripped her shoulders and turned her around. He released her to brush his fingers through the hair. The texture was lush and silky against his fingertips. The brown locks were longer than he'd thought, reaching several inches past her shoulders.

Her hair swirled and swayed in the breeze as he turned her to face him and reached for the top button of her shirt. He had it halfway undone before she slapped his hand away. "*That* is enough of your expert handling! I can unbutton my own clothes."

He stepped back to allow her more space and gave her a dubious look. "Do it then. Your dress code is right out of the Temperance League handbook." That might be true, but at the moment his attention was drawn to her hair, buffeted by the breeze. The stuff he'd dismissed as "dull brown" sparkled with auburn highlights in the setting sun, disquieting him. Taking her down a peg had him a little unsteady.

The blasted button he'd halfway dislodged opened in the stiff, sea breeze, and the Oxford cloth wagged in the wind, tormenting him with flashes of soft, pale flesh. His intention to make fun of her shifted abruptly to an uncomfortable masculine arousal. He took another step back, not to give her personal space, but to place her out of reach.

These small changes in her appearance suddenly felt like a cunning come-on. Irritated, he reminded himself that *he* had made those changes to annoy and ruffle her, not to turn himself on. Mentally shaking himself to get his head on straight, he indicated her with a dismissive wave. "You're never going to get an applicant to accept your husband position unless you sell yourself." His voice sounded gruff in his ears. He was sorry he'd started his I'm-such-an-expert prank. He didn't know who was suffering more, her or him. "A smart woman shows a sexy hint of what the man's getting."

Jen tossed her head, all the better to show off that shiny, velvety hair. Did she know what that little act of defiance did to him? "You think I should do a striptease," she demanded, eyes flashing. "Are you suggesting all men carry their brains in their trousers?"

"Don't kid yourself, darling." *Darling? He'd never called a female darling in his life.* He cleared his throat, forging on with the lesson, though it had lost any semblance of entertainment. "Men are visual creatures." *Too damn true!* He flinched as her flapping blouse caught the wind and billowed to expose the lacy edge of her bra. He forced his gaze to her sparking eyes. "You can offer all the dental, medical and retirement benefits in the world, but if you don't give out a little T and A you'll bomb."

"That shows how much you know!" she shouted. "Marriages based on mutual betterment are formed every day. My parents, as an example, are a fine-tuned machine. They have the same goals and values, are a stable couple and they've *never* been mushy or gooey over each other."

"Seeing you, I don't doubt it."

Her face tightened, her eyes glimmering with hurt. Though she was to blame for his discomfort and frustration, Cole experienced a stab of guilt for that last dig. It had been unfair. But it drove him crazy how she could stand there and be so sterile about something so fraught with intimacy and emotion as marriage.

She blinked back threatening tears, her expression turning obstinate. "I don't know why I'm bothering to tell you this, but if you insist on emotionalism, my grandmother and grandfather's history proves my point. Grandma was a widow with two small boys and no income. Grandpa was a widower with a farm to run. They got married out of mutual need. To make a long story short, they had four more children. One was my dad. And somewhere along the way, they fell madly in love. Grandma and Grandpa became the gooiest couple I've ever seen."

She shoved wind-tossed hair out of her face, her features rebellious. "So, for your information, Mr. Noone, love can grow between two people with mutual beliefs and goals, *if* they work at it. I think that kind of love is much more—more trustworthy, more *genuine* than blind, irrational hysteria! Besides, I..." She hesitated, then shook her head. "That's all I intend to say on the subject."

He wondered what she'd left unsaid, but shrugged it off. "You seem to have it all figured out."

She eyed him with obvious skepticism, as though she

didn't believe he was convinced. "I'm not a person who does things without great thought."

"And you're planning to have children with this man?" That was a question he hadn't expected to ask. But now that he had, he was curious about the answer.

Her lips parted with shock at his bluntness, but she regained herself and nodded. "If it's any of your business, yes. I want children."

He couldn't believe it. Here she was advertising for a husband to gain a promotion, and she had the temerity to suggest she planned to bring children into the scheme, too? "How deluded can you be?" he demanded. "An educated, intelligent, successful man is not likely to defer his career to become your wife and nanny. Maybe you'd better stick to men of retirement age who'll be willing to stay home with junior. Or find some terminally employment-challenged guy who can't hold on to a good job."

"Like you, for instance?" she retorted.

Before he could respond she whirled away and stomped off. Cole watched her go, reluctantly admiring her spirit. The dancing highlights in her hair and the hint of soft curve beneath the Temperance League attire gave him a rough time. He not only found Miss Sancroft full of spirit, but troublingly sexy, even with all her starched primness and narcissistic plotting.

Turning away, he strode toward the peace and solitude of his cabin. He stuffed his hands into his jeans' pockets, annoyed that they still tingled from the touch of her hair. "I'd be better off on my yacht—with some willing girlfriend," he muttered. "I'm obviously overworked and under—" He ground out a raw oath.

Jen couldn't help the fact that the bothersome Mister Fix-it was outside, behind his cabin, barbecuing on a charcoal grill. She couldn't help it that he could see the deck of the big house from where he stood, or that he would have a clear view of her when she hurried down the steps and scurried across the lawn. Or an even better view when she darted through the fence and bounded over the grassy dunes to the beach.

She couldn't help any of that. She needed to get out of what she was beginning to think of as the "house of rejection." To restore her positive attitude it was imperative she experience the calming splash of the surf, the brine-tinged breeze, take in the restful sight of a majestic orange sun as it set.

She took a deep breath and yanked open the back door planning to pay no heed to this man and make it to the beach with as little fuss as possible. The success of her plan was wholly dependent on her determination to ignore Cole Noone. She had never been more determined about anything in her life.

She shut the door with barely a sound, hoping Cole might be so preoccupied with charcoaling he wouldn't notice her. Quickly she aimed for the steps, hurried down them, whirled toward the fence and made a run for it. Once on the other side, she catapulted herself across the dunes, able to breathe only after her bare feet hit warm sand.

She gulped in pungent air as she swept her gaze over the azure sea. "That was easier than I thought," she mused out loud. Before she realized what she was doing, she turned to check on Cole. To her utter dismay, he was not concentrating on his cooking as she'd expected. He was looking at her. When their eyes met, he lifted his long-handled cooking fork in a silent, unsmiling acknowledgment.

Without returning his salutation she whirled away and headed down the beach in the opposite direction. Breathing deeply, she not only took in the briny air but the aroma of whatever Cole was cooking. The delicious scent made her aware of how hungry she was. Because of a mix-up in appointments, she'd had to interview through the lunch hour. And breakfast had consisted of a cup of instant coffee and a toaster tart.

Too bad Ruthie was no better at cooking than Jen. They'd ordered out every night and it was getting monotonous. What she wouldn't give for a home-cooked meal. Drat Cole! Not only must he nettle and nag her, telling her she's not just a fool, but one with *no* sex appeal, but he must tantalize her with the lip-smacking, smoky fragrance of a real, down-home Texas barbecue, grilled over mesquite coals.

As she walked along, she tried to forget how badly the day had gone. She was beginning to fear there weren't as many logical-thinking men out there as she'd assumed.

Cole's cautionary words rang in her ear. Perhaps she had been rash to think some successful man would consent to marry her and be her "housewife" of sorts, move to Dallas, share in the care of their two-point-four children and become an active partner in *her* corporate functions.

Lots of men had *wives* who devoted themselves to helping their spouses in their careers. Her mother was her dad's right arm, a full partner in *his* career, overseeing and coordinating many of the functions he had to deal with as president of a small Texas college. She kicked at the sand, annoyed that Cole may have a valid point. "I *do* need a wife," she muttered. "How dare the business world be so unfair."

An hour later, only marginally recovering from the disappointing three days of interviewing, she was a great deal hungrier. That fact was made painfully clear once she was near enough to take in the smoky fragrance of Cole's grilling. She cast a surreptitious look in the direction of the cabin and came to a halt.

Not only was Cole still there, but so was Ruthie! A card table had been set up, a colorful red-and-white checked cloth thrown over it. Three folding chairs had also been set up, one still unoccupied. She had a sinking feeling she was the person they had in mind to plant her derriere there. What a pity she was so hungry and she loved barbecue so much, or she wouldn't even consider joining them.

Her strength and resolve were at an all-time low. Even if she had the fortitude to refuse to join them, what kind of excuse could she make now? Ruthie would know she didn't have any plans, and since that third chair was there, her assistant had clearly made that plain to Cole. She shook her head, muttering, "Ruthie, you have some heavy-duty explaining to do."

What now—lie and say she had a conference call, eat another of those cardboardy breakfast tarts, slug down a tepid cup of instant coffee and call it dinner? Possibly go out to some roadside café and eat alone? Or—and this was the worst-case scenario—give in to her passion for barbecue, and join them?

The decision came quickly, since Ruthie spotted her, jumped up waving and shouting her name. There was no ignoring the woman, and Jen had no plausible excuse— even if her stomach had allowed one. She decided this would be a good time to find out how fast she could eat and run.

With a heavy heart and feet of lead, she trudged through the gate and across the lawn. The scent of barbecued chicken drew her straight to the table. From the amount of food laid out, she wouldn't be hungry for long. Baked potatoes, charred black on the outside from being cooked over coals, lay steaming in a serving bowl. A tossed salad of colorful veggies looked good enough to be immortalized in a still-life painting. Barbecued chicken pieces, piled high on a metal platter, seduced with their succulent aroma. A tall, sweaty pitcher of iced tea looked so cool and inviting, Jen wanted to dive in.

"Well, at last," Ruthie said with a wide grin, "we were afraid you'd walked into the sea."

Jen winced, hoping Ruthie hadn't been chattering to Cole about the disastrous day.

The curly headed assistant stood up and brushed crumbs off her jeans. "Time for my evening call to Raymond." She stretched out her hand to Cole. "You saved my sanity,

Noone. I swear one more take-out burger and I would have cracked up.''

"What—what…'' Jen wasn't crazy about what this looked like. "Ruthie, you're not leaving!''

Her assistant shifted to smile winningly at her boss. "You took such a long walk, and I was starving, so I went ahead and ate. Besides, you know Raymond expects my call by seven.''

"Don't you have your cell phone?'' Jen didn't care if she sounded desperate for Ruthie to stay. Cole already knew she didn't relish spending time alone with him. Especially after last night, when he'd so brazenly taken down her hair, not to mention unbuttoning…well, to say she felt awkward around him was hardly a strong enough word. Particularly since she'd reluctantly taken his advice about her clothes. Not to the extent she'd done to attract Tony. *Heaven* forbid. Still, the interviews up to now had been so disastrous, she had to face the fact that a slight compromise in hairstyle and attire was critical.

Today, she'd worn her gray cotton jumper *without* a blouse. Since the bodice dipped a little low for her comfort level, she'd found a pink and gray scarf to tie around her neck, which was not only good cleavage camouflage but added a feminine touch of color to the ensemble. Also, very reluctantly, she'd left her hair down. After the interviews were over, she'd used the scarf to tie back her hair so it wouldn't blow in her face on her walk.

Her scarf was wrapped around her head, not her neck! With that realization, Jen became very aware of her neckline, and how frightfully low it dipped. Abruptly, she tugged the scarf down around her neck to veil exposed flesh. She hoped Cole hadn't noticed. She also hoped he hadn't noticed she'd belted her slim jumper, blousing it at the waist so the hem hit her several inches above her knees.

Even with these feminizing efforts, the day had been anything but sterling. The only real difference she'd seen was that she'd had a harder time maintaining eye contact with applicants, since they tended to ogle her legs, crossed at her exposed knees. She still couldn't believe all men were Cole Noone's type when it came to "what men like in a woman," but today's batch seemed to be.

"I left my phone in the house," Ruthie said, drawing Jen back. "Besides, you don't want to hear Ray and me talk. When we're apart more than two nights, we tend to have a lot of phone sex."

Jen could feel her cheeks go hot, and she couldn't think of a thing to say. Cole's laugh was troublingly sexy, but Jen managed to keep her mortified gaze on her assistant. Ruthie winked at her boss then gave the bounteous table a wave. "Supper's delicious. I told Cole he could barbecue for me anytime." She threw her host a playful kiss. "'Bye, you lifesaver."

He nodded a cheerful goodbye, grinning at her as she sauntered off. After a moment his attention shifted to Jen. That jolted her, making her realize she'd been watching him.

As he took her in his smile disappeared. "You look— almost woman-like today."

She didn't know why her heart was suddenly racing. It couldn't be the fact that she was standing across the table from a provokingly handsome man. She hoped it wasn't that, since he thought of her as "almost woman-like." Ever since Tony, she'd fought frivolous feelings about men, and she'd been successful. What was it about this man who could insult her and still cause her pulse to gallop like a racehorse? "*Almost* woman-*like*," she repeated, trying for flip. "Mr. Cole, have you ever heard of the phrase, 'Damning with faint praise'?"

He relaxed back in his chair, crossing his arms over the everlastingly bare chest. *Did the man own a shirt!* "I've heard lots of phrases." He nodded toward the empty chair. "Park yourself. You look worn down."

She swallowed, wishing she had the wherewithal to stomp off. But she was so hungry, and the food looked so good. The fight went out of her as if he'd pricked her with a pin. She sank into the offered chair and sagged back to stare up at the tree branches above them. "Okay, I'm too tired to argue and too hungry to have any pride."

She didn't know what went on for the next couple of seconds, for he didn't speak and she didn't hear any movement. The surf boomed off in the distance and a seagull cried plaintively. She knew exactly how it felt.

"Dark meat or light?" he asked. She heard a thud and sensed that he'd moved the chicken platter.

She glanced his way. "Any drumsticks left?"

He held the platter up for her to scan. She picked up a nearby leg. Before he could replace the tray on the table, she grabbed one more. Without commenting, he handed her the other dishes one at a time so she could serve herself. She began to eat and he poured her a glass of tea. Still he said nothing. After a slow count of sixty, she couldn't stand the suspense and shifted her focus from her food to him.

He sat there, arms crossed, his expression speculative, his eyes on her.

"Oh—uh, it's very good," she said, telling the truth. Even her dad's barbecued chicken couldn't match this for flavor and juiciness. She had to give Cole credit. He might be a meddling pain, but he was a marvelous cook.

He lifted his chin in a half nod to acknowledge her compliment, but he didn't respond. She experienced a prickle of apprehension wondering what he was thinking during all his silent study of her.

She took several bites of the salad, finished her baked potato. Then ate a chicken leg, and still he watched her. The wind whipped up, the air heavy with foreboding. With each bite she took and every second that ticked by, Jen found it harder and harder to swallow. Her ears began to ring with anxiety. Finally, unable to bear the stress, she plunked her fork to her plate and faced him. "I can't eat if you keep staring at me like that. Whatever it is, just say it!"

He observed her unblinking for another beat, then shook his head. "I'm baffled. What job could possibly justify advertising for a husband? Why do you feel you have to be married to get your promotion?" He shrugged, the casual move showing off delicious muscle in his chest and shoulders. "Don't you have faith in your own merit?"

She'd reached the ragged edge of a very tough day, and this was the final straw. She planted her fists on the table and pushed up, overturning her chair. It fell to the grass with a dull thud. "Of course, I have faith in my own merit!"

She leaned on the flats of her hands, bending aggressively toward him. Her hair frolicked in the breeze, and for a moment he disappeared behind the undulating curtain of brown. She tossed her head to clear her vision. "My problem is not my merit! I work for a conservative firm and I have a very uptight boss. He's the reason for all this, because to get my promotion, he's the one I have to satisfy!"

"I see." Cole looked dubious. "And what does being married have to do with it?"

"Everything!" she said, warming to the subject. She'd held her truest, deepest feelings in for so long, her bitterness came flooding out with a vengeance. It felt good to finally vent! "Because my boss is a stick-in-the-mud jerk out of the dark ages, who doesn't promote unmarried people to the presidency!"

"Presidency?" He quirked an eyebrow; his surprise and incredulity galled her.

"Yes, presidency!" she said. "Don't look so shocked. I may be a woman, even a relatively young woman, but I'm extremely good at what I do, and I deserve to be the president!"

She eyed him unwaveringly, a lethal calm descending upon her. Her mind was suddenly clear, her attitude earnest and full of passion. "When I set a goal, I take aim and I don't look back. Sure what I'm doing has risks, but nothing in life worth anything comes without risks!'' She straightened, feeling better than she had in days.

Her resolve was stronger than ever, her optimism revived. "You've called me stupid in more ways than one. Well, a wise philosopher once said, 'If you want to improve, be content to be thought foolish and stupid.''' She eyed him with deadly resolve. "To get what I want—what I'm *entitled* to—I'm absolutely willing." She lowered her voice. "Any more questions?''

He looked skeptical, but she didn't care. Let him think she was the biggest nutcase ever born! She knew what she had to do, and it didn't matter whether *anybody* agreed with her—especially this presumptuous handyman!

"Just one more question," he said as he knelt to retrieve her chair. "Mind telling me who this unenlightened jerk is?''

"Oh—some old coot named J. C. Barringer."

Cole stilled on one knee, glancing her way. His look was too brief to grasp on an intellectual level, but it stopped her cold. A strange flash in his eyes affected her deep inside— an instinctive, disquieting prickle she couldn't comprehend.

CHAPTER FOUR

COLE finished righting her chair, using that time to assimilate her statement. Ever since she'd said the promotion was for the "presidency" he'd sensed the truth—that the "boss" she'd badmouthed for days was none other than the man who'd just fed her dinner.

Him.

Now he recalled why he remembered her name. She was one of the vice presidents of the little accounting firm that had been one of his father's holdings. He recalled his secretary mentioning that she'd sent out the notifications that he would be interviewing them in June for the top job. He'd barely begun to review their résumés before the blasted hostile takeover bid came up. He'd been forced to put the D.A.A. presidency on a back shelf in his mind, to be dealt with later. It was a small firm, little more than a blip on his corporate radar. But it had been a particular favorite of his father's, and choosing the right president deserved his best attention.

Well, he'd had close to a week on the coast to restore himself. It hadn't been enough, considering his odd insomnia lately. Still, it was evident that "later" had arrived with a vengeance.

He stood up, indicating her chair. "Calm down, Miss Sancroft. Finish your dinner." He took his seat, glanced her way. She remained standing, her color high.

The scarf about her neck waved, caught by the breeze, sliding back to hug her neck. The view revealed by the shifting silk was too stimulating for a man who'd been preoccupied with the recent passing of his father and the pressures of work. He cleared his throat, elevating his attention to her face. "What's the name of the company?" he asked, though he already knew the answer.

She pursed her lips, possibly trying to rein in her passion. He was sorry to see it, since she was quite a vision when she was passionate. That thought tried to push forward to the next logical step—passionate at work, passionate at play. Images crowded into his mind, of pale skin and rumpled sheets, green eyes ablaze with desire. Of tendrils of chestnut-brown hair spread across his pillow as moist, sexy lips caressed his skin.

His gut clenched and he forced the images from his head. Rubbing his eyes, he told himself to straighten up. When he looked at her again, she was still standing. "*Hell*, sit down! You're giving me a stiff neck." That statement was at least half true, though it had nothing to do with his neck.

She blinked at his barked command but didn't immediately plunk herself into the chair. She shifted her shoulders, took a deep breath, smoothed her slender skirt then finally, slowly returned to her seat. The lamentable thing about her unhurried acquiescence was the fact that once sitting, her low-cut bodice came into his direct view. He had a strong urge to reach over and tug the scarf down to veil the taunting, feminine flesh. He resisted, knowing such a move would mortify her to the point she'd jump up and leave. He couldn't allow that. Not yet.

Lifting his tumbler he removed his glance to the amber liquid. "What's the name of the company?" he repeated, then took a long slug of the iced beverage.

"Dallas Accounting Associates."

He put down his glass and faced her, keeping his attention focused on her solemn features. He could almost understand her dilemma now. D.A.A. was hardly the largest of his holdings. It had an excellent reputation, and was notoriously conservative.

The presidency had always been given to married, settled men. That was true. Cole saw why she might feel angry and indignant. He even understood why she might jump to the conclusion that a young, single female didn't have a chance at the top job. Depending on how indignant, angry and determined she was, she might react aggressively, even drastically, since the presidency of the respected, up-and-coming company would be a coup for someone half again her age.

What she didn't understand was that Albert Barringer had not been a close-minded old coot. His choices for the presidency had been restricted to married men solely because, in his opinion, they'd been the best choices at the time. Perhaps, two years ago when the last president was chosen, Albert Barringer thought she needed more seasoning. It certainly wasn't because he was the chauvinist pig she thought he was.

"An accounting firm?" he said at last, deciding on a generic response for now. He wasn't ready to relinquish the part of "handyman." Now that he knew he was the "old coot" she desperately wanted to satisfy, his impromptu masquerade had become more involved, but he decided to give himself time to absorb everything before telling her who he was. He still felt it was absurd to find a husband the way she was doing it, and wrong for the reason she was doing it, but he could at least see why she might be desperate enough to try.

No matter her reason, no matter that he might understand a little better her desperation, the fact remained she was bent on using some man to feather her career nest. His animosity surged. "I still say marriage for a promotion is wrong."

She broke eye contact, picked up her fork and stabbed at bits of salad vegetables. Her face tight, eyes bright with emotion, she muttered, "I can't talk to you. You couldn't possibly understand."

"Really?" He sat back and eyed her with derision. "What if I told you my mother used my father to get ahead?"

She looked dubious and lay her fork aside to put all her energies into glaring at him. "I would be very skeptical."

He continued to watch her, allowing his animosity to show. "She didn't marry my father, but when she got pregnant with his child she bartered her baby son away for her own promotion, of sorts. My father took me in, raised me, loved me, but he never got over her."

He saw something flicker deep in her eyes. They clouded with hazy sadness, as though his remark sparked some difficult memory. She swallowed, turned away, nodding vaguely, as though reliving some pain of her own. "I'm—I'm sorry for your father."

Cole sat forward, leaned toward Jen, experiencing a twinge of concern. "What is it?"

She refused to face him, shaking her head. "Nothing."

He frowned, wondering at the change in her, the show of vulnerability. It touched him, taking the edge off his outrage. "I watched my father suffer in silence all the rest of his life because of a selfish woman." Unable to deal with the view of her low-cut bodice one second longer, he reached out, hooked her scarf with a finger and tugged it down to hide her cleavage. "So, don't tell me I couldn't possibly understand, Miss Sancroft. I understand all too well."

She flicked him a glance, her eyes liquid and large. He couldn't tell if it had been his speech or the realization that her breasts had been practically laid bare before him that caused her mortification. She cleared her throat, hastily looking away. "I—I'm sorry about your father," she murmured. "Sorry your mother was—was such a…"

"Cold-blooded witch?" he finished gravely.

She avoided his eyes and with a shaky hand retrieved her fork. He observed her as she picked at her food.

"I'll tell you one thing," he went on, gruffly. "When—and if—I marry, it won't be for anything less than the truest, deepest kind of love. From both parties."

She blinked several times as though trying to get her

emotions under control. "I wish you luck," she murmured almost too softly for him to hear. "Believe me, I know how cruel—I mean, well..." She flicked him a solemn look before returning her gaze to her plate. "I'm not going to *use* anybody. My motives are perfectly honorable."

He watched her, his emotions mixed. He was annoyed at her for her die-hard insistence on the husband-snaring scheme. At the same time, he felt an urge to take her in his arms and comfort her for the stark unhappiness he'd glimpsed in her eyes.

That night, alone in his cottage, Cole considered Jennifer Sancroft's actions and possible motives from every angle. He checked his computer e-mails, studying attached documents containing the job histories of all three vice presidents. He took several hours to scrutinize each candidate's résumé and corporate records.

As he read, he had to admit her qualifications were top-notch. She was a brilliant business woman and had never lost an audit to the Internal Revenue Service. She'd brought wealthy clients to the firm and clearly had dedicated herself to her career. Former bosses called her an ingenious dynamo with the drive of ten men.

Cole had seen glimpses of that in her single-minded determination these past three days. She was set on using some man to get her promotion, and too wrapped up in the urgency of the process and quaint family folklore to see it for the blunder it was. As far as he was concerned, that was a big flaw.

He wrestled with what to do, how to handle this new twist. He hated her status-seeking scheme, had seen the same kind of thing too many times in women he'd known, and a mother he never knew. Even so, Miss Sancroft had a good record, and was justly in the running. Should he allow his prejudice of women like her to affect his decision? Would it? The fact that some wayward part of him was attracted to her also preyed on his mind. Could he be impartial?

Around midnight, he faced the fact that he'd made one definite decision hours ago, when he hadn't immediately told her who he was after discovering she wanted the accounting firm's presidency. For the time being, at least, he would continue in his handyman guise. He told himself it was a good way to observe her, to rise above long-standing prejudices and study her objectively—*for the job,* he insisted—hoping he wasn't lying to himself.

"What do you mean, you're leaving?" In her shock and disbelief, Jen dropped her toaster tart on the kitchen floor. She stared in stupefaction at Ruthie, who stood in the entryway to the kitchen, a suitcase in her hand.

"I—I got a call this morning. I've been offered a job at corporate headquarters at twice my salary." She shrugged, looking sheepish and contrite. "They said they need me immediately or they'll have to get somebody else."

When the full impact of her assistant's announcement penetrated, Jen leaned weakly against the kitchen counter, feeling sick. "We've been together for five years. I didn't know you were unhappy with me."

"I'm not!" Ruthie said. "I wasn't. I've loved working for you."

"Then why did you apply for another job?"

The redhead shook her head, appearing puzzled. "I didn't. I—I don't know how my name came up. But I can't afford to turn it down."

Jen wasn't surprised that others might want Ruthie. She was an outstanding employee. Until this moment Jen hadn't realized how much she'd grown to depend on her. She'd told Ruthie things she had never told another soul. But now, with Ruthie's statement that she was leaving, the realization of how much she'd be missed, not only as an assistant but a friend, was like a huge wave crashing down on her head.

She flailed mentally and had trouble breathing. "Of

course, they'd want you," she admitted. "You're wonderful, but—but what am I going to do without you?" She looked helplessly around, trying to think. "I trust you, Ruthie! I need you! I can't interview a bunch of men about marriage—all alone!" Without much attention she reached back and lowered her mug to the counter. When pottery clanked on granite, coffee splashed on her hand. Luckily it was as tepid as it was weak, and didn't burn. But even if it had scalded her, a little blistering would be the least of her worries. "I'm practically propositioning these men. What if one of them gets—gets crazy and decides to—to sample the merchandise?"

Ruthie looked repentant, but only as repentant as somebody who'd just doubled her salary can look. "I'm really sorry, boss," she said. "You know Ray's had some setbacks at work. We need the money." With her free hand she waved toward the east. "You could ask the hunk to keep an ear out for your screams."

Jen closed her eyes, unable to believe her assistant's—correction, *ex*-assistant's—preposterous suggestion. "That's very helpful," she muttered.

"No, really. Think about it." Ruthie said. "He's huge. He's a great cook and he's not attracted to you. What more could you ask for?"

Jen frowned, preferring not to think about how pitifully accurate that recounting was. "How can you leave me just like that?"

Ruthie's face flushed. "You know I never would if we didn't need the money."

Jen exhaled, miserable and frantic. "I can't match that salary, but as a former Marine I'd think you'd understand the importance of loyalty."

Ruthie looked near tears. "That's just it." She made an apologetic face. "Ray and the kids come first. That's where my loyalty has to lie."

As much as Jen wanted to, she couldn't argue. Just because the company was her family, her first loyalty, didn't mean it had to be Ruthie's. Facing defeat, she slumped back, her gaze sinking to the floor.

She heard a honk from out front and knew the cab that would take Ruthie to the airport was there. The jarring sound brought the full, heartbreaking understanding that Ruthie was truly leaving. *Now.* In that instant she saw how selfish she was being. Ruthie deserved this opportunity. After all, considering what Jen was doing to get a better job, she had no right to be angry with her assistant for quitting to accept a new position, no matter how abruptly.

Battling to put on a good face, she forced a smile. "Look, Ruthie, don't mind me. You're doing the right thing. You'd be crazy not to take the job."

The redhead took a deep breath, and blinked back tears. Overwhelmed by the sight of Ruthie's distress, she dashed across the room and threw her arms about her friend. "I'm sorry. I'm happy for you. Really!" She squeezed hard. "Don't worry. I'll be fine." Grasping Ruthie by the arms, she stepped back and managed a real smile. "You deserve this break."

Another blast on the cab's horn split the air.

"You'd better go," Jen whispered, grateful her voice didn't break.

They shared one brief look, Ruthie's eyes shimmering with regret at having to abandon Jen. "Take care, boss," she said, her words quivering with emotion. "Promise me you'll talk to Cole."

Jen didn't dare say anything for fear her despair would show. The idea of asking for Cole's help was horrifying, but this was no time to start that debate. She merely nodded and held desperately to her smile.

Ruthie broke eye contact and turned away. A moment later she was gone.

Jen stood motionless listening to the silence. From inside she couldn't hear the surf. Couldn't hear the seagulls. When the shock began to wear off, she focused on her wristwatch. Seven-thirty. Her first appointment was at eight. Five more minutes ticked away as Jen stood there staring at nothing, her mind too numb to think straight.

When she finally roused herself, she knew she had to face Cole. In today's world it was insane to invite total strangers into your home when alone, especially to interview them for something so intimate as "husband." She had no choice but to ask him to keep an eye out for overly excited candidates. She couldn't involve anybody else.

She walked to the kitchen counter and rested heavily on her hands, hesitating. Cole already knew everything. He was there, and he was, as Ruthie said, huge. He would certainly be an intimidating presence. And, as Ruthie also pointed out, he had no amorous interest in her. He'd made that clear. He hadn't quite called her a dog, but he'd called her priggish—among other things.

Having him around all the time was an unsettling thought. Ever since she'd first spotted him painting the fence she'd had to continually remain on the alert. No one since Tony had affected her so intensely on an emotional level. That frightened her. Cole Noone, handyman, might be talented with his hands, cook masterfully and be thoughtful enough to offer a person iced tea on a hot day, but he was not what she was looking for in a mate. She would find a compatible husband in a responsible, controlled environment, using logic and reason. It was a shame she would have to do it practically joined at the hip with a sexy hunk.

Facing that unhappy fact, Jen vowed to resist the dangerous thrill of gazing into his eyes. She promised herself to fight the ripples of excitement that raced along her spine at the sight of his bare chest. How fortunate for her current situation that he found her totally sexless. The pathetic truth was, her virtue would be safe with him.

She checked her watch. Twenty minutes until today's first applicant arrived. She had to shake herself out of this depressed stupor and deal with the situation. Inhaling for strength, she pushed away from the counter and headed to the back door. She had no choice but to ask Cole for his help, so she might as well get on with it.

Far too quickly she reached the cabin. She opened the screened door and stepped onto the porch. With great reluctance, her steps halting, she crossed a plank floor, painted cool, pale blue. She knocked on the front door, the same pale shade.

Too quickly for her calming breaths to take effect, the door swung wide. Cole towered there, once again shirtless. Fighting off an appreciative tingle, her glance skittered away to note his freshly washed jeans and scuffed work boots. Her attention bounced up to his hair, enticingly mussed, as though he hadn't gotten around to combing it. The seductive, teddy-bear image he presented was too arousing for her state of mind, and she tried to steel herself against its effect.

His expression was unreadable. She thought he'd be surprised to see her at his door, but he didn't appear to be. Standing there half naked, a piece of toast in one hand, he looked neither shocked nor puzzled.

The smell of breakfast wafted around her, bacon, eggs and rich, strong coffee. She realized with some distress that she was hungry. Her breakfast tart lay in a crumbled, seeping pile on her kitchen floor.

In the extended silence, his expression closed slightly. "I gather you're not here to sell Girl Guide cookies?"

She bit her lower lip, determined to keep her poise. It had been a bad morning, and his bothersome charisma was difficult to deal with in her emotionally tattered state. After a few heartbeats, she said, "Ruthie left. She got a job offer she couldn't refuse."

He didn't reply, so she reluctantly met his gaze and went on. "Look, here's the deal. I'm going to be alone over there—with strange men—and I thought I might..." The sentence died. She tried again. "I mean, I might run into trouble if..." She swallowed then shook her head, working to find the right words. "What I'm trying to say is, I know you think I'm totally—uh—unappealing, but if I run into somebody who *doesn't*, I might need—help."

She made herself hold eye contact, but it wasn't easy. He continued to scrutinize her, his expression inquisitive, giving her no hope he understood her plea. A headache began to work its way up from the base of her skull. She floundered around in her head to find another way to put it, hoping she could keep her voice level and placid when she did.

"I'm—I'm—um…" She ran a hand through her hair. She'd left it loose again. Now, considering Ruthie's defection, she was beginning to rethink her attempt to appear more feminine. "You see, Cole…" She feared the quiver in her voice might be audible before she got the request said. "Without Ruthie, I'll be—"

"I get it, Miss Sancroft," he interrupted. "You're asking me to hang around the house and run interference in case some guy jumps you." He took a bite of toast, watching her with those pale blue eyes. Finally, he said, "Do you want a cup of coffee?"

The aroma wafting onto the porch smelled so much better than the instant decaf she'd made, but if she was too embarrassed and nervous to maintain eye contact, how would she contemplate sharing a coffee break with him? She backed up, shaking her head, planning a quick exit as soon as she got his answer. "No—the first applicant will be here in a few minutes."

He nodded, but remained silent. His expression didn't grant her even the barest semblance of reassurance that he would agree to her request.

She felt ill. The whispering rush of surf did its best to ease her frustration. The soothing sounds, usually so tranquilizing, didn't work. It was becoming increasingly difficult to appear composed, but she had to know, had to ask, "Well—will you or won't you?"

The seconds took hours to tick by before he spoke. "I

thought liberated women of today prided themselves in not leaning on men.''

So, his answer was *no!* She should have known. Just another plain-spoken reminder she was unwelcome and unwanted. It was his scornful way of saying, if she was too afraid to carry on alone he would do whatever it took— *including nothing*—to help her leave.

She experienced a flare of anger. ''I promise, leaning on *you* is the last thing I care to do. It's just that I'm out of pepper spray.''

''Why, Miss Sancroft,'' he said, an eyebrow lifting in wry speculation. ''Are you coming on to me?''

Baffled by the remark, she asked, ''Pardon?''

''Your lack of pepper spray. Is that your idea of an invitation?''

His mockery stung and she groped for an appropriately stinging remark. Nothing pithy came to mind, but the fire of a blush heated her face. ''Mr. Noone, I—I not only would *never* come on to you, I wouldn't even accept your head on a silver platter!''

He crossed his arms over his chest. Muscle flexed as he moved, causing something inside her to clench like a fist. How dare she be attracted to this taunting brute! Angry at herself, she cried, ''If you want my opinion, I think you're a crude, sarcastic, insensitive barbarian.''

She was not rewarded with the spectacle of him crumpling beneath the heel of her insult. His scrutinizing expression did not change. On the verge of tears, she spun to go, but found her wrist captured in his grasp. ''I've had very little experience at being a bodyguard, Miss Sancroft.'' He casually looked her over before adding, ''But in your case, I think I can handle it.''

She gaped, wounded, her emotions rampaging in all directions. He was offering to help because he thought she had so little sex appeal he wouldn't have to physically restrain any overzealous husband candidates.

She desperately wanted to refuse him, tell him she could

handle the situation by herself. Though she didn't actually own pepper spray, she supposed she could hide a bottle of bug repellent between the sofa cushions. A squirt in an attacker's face might deter him long enough for her to run. Stubborn pride winning out over good judgment, she jerked free of his hold. "I would rather walk barefoot over hot coals than accept your help!"

"Okay, okay," he said, sounding vaguely amused. "You talked me into it."

She had whirled away in a huff. *What did he say?* Confused, she grew still and peered at him over her shoulder. "What?"

He shrugged, rippling more delectable muscle. "Things need fixing in the house. You've been in my way." He watched her, his gaze unwavering. "No offense."

She knew he meant to offend, but no matter how badly she wanted to tell him to go jump in the ocean, her ability to see reason had returned. It was better to be safe than sorry. Turning away, she muttered, "Yeah—sure."

The day progressed with agonizing slowness. Cole was true to his word. Shortly after the first meeting started he arrived via the front door in full view of the interviewee. Jen noted the applicant's apprehensive expression when he saw Cole, big, bare-chested, brandishing a nail gun. Cole announced his arrival and said he'd be there all day. In the process he drilled the job-seeker with a look that stated, *I'll nail your rear to the floor if you accost the lady.*

Unfortunately, every time his gaze touched hers, his message was equally eloquent in its disapproval. After he made his gorilla-like appearance for each new candidate, he went about making repairs, his testosterone-drenched banging from somewhere inside the house reverberating through the interviews—a constant reminder that she had a very grudging bodyguard on the premises.

Jen's emotions on the subject of Cole's nearness fluctuated from thankful to mortified. On one hand, she appreciated his "I Am A Bloodthirsty Beast" act—not that he was *acting*. On the other, every time he happened by, she lost her train of thought. She would catch sight of him, flaunting his muscle-rippling, tough-guy-ness, then she'd transfer her attention to her current husband applicant and the comparison cast a pall over her whole project.

Sometimes, when the interviewee was not physically appetizing or fell short on career credentials, she had to restrain herself from throwing up her hands and running out the door to put distance between herself and the thoroughly unsuitable handyman. She had to continually remind herself that Cole had *no* credentials—well, at least as far as an impressive job résumé. On the up side, his Mister Fix-it job wouldn't keep him flying hither and yon on business. He'd be available to cook, keep the home in good repair, and most importantly care for the children.

Children.

Her stomach fluttered with feminine excitement, but as quickly as the erotic notion materialized, she reminded herself what foolishness it was. Rubbing her knuckles over her eyes to banish the erotic image, she muttered, "No—no, Jennifer! That's crazy!"

"Excuse me?" The latest job-seeker sounded put out. "Well, lady, if you ask me, you're the one who's crazy."

Yanked back to reality, she realized the man had pushed up from the sofa. "I'm outta here."

She stood, "Mr. uh…" His name slipped her mind. She scanned her notes. Powell. "Mr. Powell. I wasn't speaking to you. Please, forgive me for—"

"Forget it, lady." He stalked around the couch and headed for the exit. A short, stout man, he was a blur of brown. Brown hair, brown suit, brown shoes. Even his tie was brown.

Jen told herself appearance didn't matter, and she tried to feel that way. In truth, Mr. Powell's manner was what really counted against him. From the moment he'd walked through the door, his attitude had been insolent, not to mention a hair-trigger temper. As far as career assets, he was unemployed and his track record was spotty at best. She was sure his inferior résumé fed his belligerence. He expected to be rejected so he took the offensive. It was a shame he couldn't see that his self-doubt and insecurity were his own worst enemies. Those shortcomings, of course, were fatal flaws as far as her requirements for a mate—even if he *hadn't* told her she was crazy.

More relieved than distressed by his testy departure, she followed him to offer a polite farewell. "Well, I appreciate your—"

With an ear-splitting boom the door slammed shut. Shell-shocked, she stared at the etched glass in the door. "It was nice meeting you, too," she muttered.

She heard footsteps approaching along the entry hall and squeezed her eyes shut. She did *not* need this right now.

"That didn't take long." Cole sounded too close.

She counted to ten to gather her poise. "Don't," she warned, not in the mood to be taunted. "Just—*don't!*" She made herself turn around, show him he was not dealing with a defeated failure. When she faced him, she berated herself for the thousandth time for finding him so physically magnificent. Sadly, there was no other word for him. He had the kind of face and body you would expect to find carved in marble in an ancient Greek temple glorifying masculine beauty. So terribly unfair.

He stood there, tall, powerfully built, his stunning gaze intent on her. She shook off the hypnotic effect and made herself check the time. "Look, it's nearly five. Mr. Powell was the last interview today." She met his eyes. "You can go." She felt a smattering of comfort at making a managerial decision. It gave her a feeling of having some control, on a day that hadn't been good for feeling in control.

Cole's lips pursed suspiciously, as though he was laughing at her attempt to boss him around. Her sense of being in control evaporated, but she tried not to deflate physically. After another tick of the clock, he inclined his head in a slight salute. "Yes, ma'am." He lifted his nail gun, indicating it. "I'll just get the rest of my tools."

She stood very erect. With a nod, she bluffed authority, as though giving her permission made a speck of difference. "Go ahead."

He headed for the kitchen. As soon as he was gone, she sagged against the entry wall, limp as a rag. She was so weary, losing hope of finding any husband candidate both adequate and willing. Her hope of finding somebody who was actually appealing grew depressingly dim.

After a moment she heard the back door open, then shut. She closed her eyes, relieved. Cole was gone.

A second later her eyes popped wide with a jarring realization.

Tomorrow he would be back.

CHAPTER FIVE

JEN was too restless to sit inside and munch her peanut butter and strawberry jam sandwich. She took it outside with her and ambled along the beach, barefoot, trying not to wonder where Cole might be. She hadn't seen him when she'd peeked toward the cottage. She told herself that was a good thing. She didn't have any desire to have him scowl at her while she ate. She didn't need an ulcer!

Weary and dejected, she drifted along the sand, munching the gummy, overly-sweet concoction. Movement caught her eye and she shifted her attention in time to see a duck flutter to the sand not far away. She smiled at it, then her smile faded. Something was wrong. She could tell by the way it held its little head. It quacked at her, and she noticed it couldn't seem to close its bill all the way.

"Oh, my..." she said, realizing what was wrong. The poor little thing had a fish hook in its bill. "Oh, my goodness." She didn't know what to do. Her parents had never had pets in their home, so she'd never had any. With her complete lack of experience, she wasn't sure how to help. She tore off strips of crust and tossed them toward the duck. "Here, honey," she whispered. "Don't be afraid."

The little mallard waddled up to the first piece of crust and struggled to eat it but had difficulty getting the bread into its bill, with the big hook in the way. Jen experienced a rush of panic. The poor thing would starve. Unable to think of anything else to try, she squatted down, holding out a strip of crust. "Come here, baby," she coaxed, thinking maybe she could help get the food past the hook. But what about tomorrow and the next day?

She winced, feeling helpless. It would die if it couldn't

eat. She was amazed when it gradually came closer, quacking and attempting to pick up bits of crust. A few strips made it down the little duck's throat, but only if its head was turned just right and gravity could take over.

When it got close enough, Jen lunged and grabbed it, getting a loud, frightened squawk for her effort. "I'm not going to hurt you, sweetie," she cooed. "But—but I have to hold on to you while I try to get the hook out." Unfortunately, holding the duck took both her arms. Now what was she going to do?

The duck flapped and squawked and Jen floundered in her mind, scared but determined. "Just—just calm down. I'll think of something." She cuddled the duck to her breast, trying to soothe it with her gentle voice. "Don't—don't be afraid. I'm scared enough for us both."

"What are you doing?" came a masculine voice.

For once Jen was beside herself with joy at the sound of Cole's arrival. She whirled. "Oh—thank goodness." She indicated the duck. "It has a hook in its bill and I don't have enough hands to hold it and remove the hook, too."

Cole stood there, wordlessly, taking in the sight—a squawking, squirming, frightened little bird and an awkward heroine, clearly as inexperienced with small animals as she was with men. After a momentary pause during which Jen preferred not to dwell on what he might be thinking, he glanced down at his tool belt, slipped a pliers-like gadget from a slot and walked forward.

"What are you going to do?" she asked.

"You hold her. I'll snip the hook with these wire cutters and pull it out."

"Oh, right." Jen bit down on her lip and held on to the little brown duck as securely as she could, praying she wouldn't injure it in the process.

Cole nipped the hook's barbed point off and pulled the severed metal out, freeing the bird. "Good as new, young lady." He stuck the broken pieces of the hook in a leather pouch on his belt and returned the tool to its place.

Jen stood very still, clutching the duck.

He smiled crookedly at her. "You can put her down," he said. "The operation is over."

"Oh—right." His assurance brought her out of her strange stupor. She lowered the duck to the sand where it immediately went about devouring the scraps of sandwich. "Poor thing must have been hungry."

"She'll be thirsty, too. I'll get her some fresh water."

"Oh…" Jen lifted her gaze to meet his. "Right. Water."

He watched her for a long moment. "You never had a pet, did you?"

She shook her head. "No."

He glanced down at the duck, then back at her. "That makes what you did extraordinarily nice."

Before she absorbed his soft compliment he'd hopped over the fence and was halfway to his cabin.

She stared after him, feeling unaccountably buoyant. A moment later he disappeared into the cottage, quickly reappearing carrying a bowl. She noticed he'd taken off the tool belt.

She walked to the fence. "I'll take the bowl."

"Thanks." He handed it to her. "Put it down nearby. She'll find it."

As he jumped back over the fence, Jen did as he suggested then faced him, her heart fluttering strangely. He thought she had done something nice—*extraordinarily* nice. She felt the urge to smile and didn't resist. "You had pets?" she asked.

"All kinds. Dogs, birds, cats. Even a snake, once."

"My mother is allergic to fur and feathers." She shook her head in wonder. "I never thought of having a snake for a pet."

He broke eye contact to watch the duck waddle to the water bowl and drink. When he looked at her again, he smiled, seemingly satisfied about the duck's recovery. "The idea of having a pet snake doesn't horrify you?"

She shrugged. "Not really."

His smile didn't dim but seemed to spread to his eyes. "You surprise me, Miss Sancroft." He indicated the beach with a wave. "I was going for a walk. You're welcome to come along."

His casual invitation astonished her and she didn't know what to think. Maybe he was very forgiving when it came to people who cared about animals. She fought an internal battle, wanting very much to walk with him. But was it wise? She seemed to be more emotional about Cole than she wanted to be about any man. Hadn't she learned that lesson? Somehow she sensed Cole wouldn't be the lying cheat Tony was, but even if he were a nice man, he wasn't the sort of mate she was looking for.

Very reluctantly, she shook her head. "I—I have some—thing I need to do. But—thanks."

He pursed his lips, then nodded. "Okay." He turned away and moved off along the beach. A few seconds later the dowdy brown mallard waggled by. Jen followed it with her eyes, realizing with some surprise it was trailing Cole. Every third or fourth step it quacked, as though calling after him.

Her attention trailed from the mallard to Cole. He strolled along, his gait elegant, yet completely male. She had difficulty taking her eyes off him. It suddenly occurred to her she hadn't thanked him for all he'd done for her today. She owed Cole Noone—big-time. She knew it, and he knew it. She hoped she wasn't rationalizing in her desire to follow him, be near him. That would be truly stupid. Nevertheless, she headed in his direction. When she reached the duck, waddling toward Cole, she gave it a side-long look. "How shallow can you be? Shame on you for allowing yourself to be seduced by magnetic blue eyes and a fit physique."

"What?"

She winced and glanced his way. Only a couple of body lengths up the beach, he halted and turned, his expression questioning. Had he heard? She threw up a prayer that he hadn't and fibbed, "I—was telling the duck that we both owed you." He didn't respond, so either he believed her or he'd decided not to call her a liar to her face. Hurrying past the duck, she caught up with him.

"Hey, Cole..." She reached out and touched his wrist. He peered at her, his expression skeptical. "Thank you for today." She tried out a smile. Amazingly, it felt absolutely natural. She hadn't realized she could produce a naturally occurring smile during this stressful time, especially not at him. "Could I offer you dinner?" Where had that invitation come from? The idea of cooking for him hadn't entered her head—at least not on any conscious level. Consciously she'd thought maybe she could pay him a small salary. Say fifty dollars a day for his bodyguard duty, but dinner? She remembered the peanut butter and jelly sandwich and blanched. What did she even have to feed him?

His wrist was warm and sturdy under her fingers. An insidious flutter of attraction in her belly set off an internal alarm, and she abruptly released him. Her gaze rose to his, and she could see doubt in his eyes.

"You want to make dinner for me?" he asked.

She experienced a wave of apprehension. What if he accepted? What could she offer him? A peanut butter sandwich would be an insult, and she had nothing else that could be termed "dinner." She didn't think toaster tarts qualified. "I—well—"

"I thought you couldn't cook."

Whether he meant to hurt her or not, that stung. She clasped her hands together to rid herself of the stimulating feel of his skin. "I admit, I'm hardly a gourmet." She forced herself to hold his gaze. "But, well, I'd like to thank you for today." She looked away, embarrassed to have to say it. "And—er—for when you come back tomorrow—and all."

"I'm sure you mean well," he said. Suspecting a "but" was coming, she couldn't help but face him. A part of her hoped for a "but," yet another side of her, a crazy, disobedient side, already mourned his looming rejection. "I have a—date," he finished.

She felt the impact of his statement in the pit of her stomach, like the kick of a Texas bull. Though she had sensed the rejection was coming, she didn't dream his reason would be a date. *Why not, silly woman?* she berated herself inwardly. *Why wouldn't such a gorgeous man have a girlfriend, or several girlfriends? Just because your life is sterile and solitary doesn't mean his has to be.*

Why did his revelation dismay her so? "A date," she repeated, as though needing to hear it from her own lips. Crossing her arms at her waist, she attempted to look casual and self-assured. "No matter. Some other time, then?"

"It's not necessary, Miss Sancroft."

Annoyance flooded through her. It was no longer possible to let him reject her. She'd had so much rejection this week, she couldn't take any more. "I think it *is* necessary, Mr. Noone," she retorted. "Let's say tomorrow night?"

He watched her for a tense moment before he graced her with a stirring smile. "Well—if it's necessary." He nodded. "I accept."

Why couldn't she breathe? Flustered, thrilled and terrified to her core, she broke eye contact and stared toward the sea. "Fine."

"Good night, then."

She couldn't move, couldn't turn to acknowledge his departure, though all her senses zeroed in on the crunch of his boots as they moved across the sand. She also became aware that the quacking noise receded as the duck waddled after her hero.

Jen continued to look out to sea, not quite believing what had just happened. She'd actually made a dinner date with Cole Noone. What had possessed her? Had all the frustration and disappointment of this past week made her psychotic? Or had that one small but wholly unexpected compliment scrambled her brain. Good Lord, he'd called her "extraordinarily nice" and she'd become a blithering idiot—shades of that scary pink fog made her go weak at the knees. How many times had she warned herself against spending more time than absolutely necessary with the man?

She found herself turning to stare after him as he headed through the gate. He halted before closing it to allow the duck to waddle through. How sweet. *How sweet?*

Had she actually thought *that?* She whirled away. Cool water rushed across her feet and she looked down at the bubbling surf.

She needed to walk, to think. Tomorrow was Friday, the end of her first week of interviewing. She'd thought by now she'd have at least one passable candidate.

Shoving her hands into her skirt pockets she tramped through the shallow surf as it splashed against her ankles. Cole's face flashed in her mind, a vision that made her catch her breath. Why did he have to be the most exhilarating man who'd set foot inside the beach house all week?

Not only was he the most exciting male she'd run across, in her search or out of it. He'd told her the hard truth about what men wanted in a woman. No matter how backhanded and insulting the advice, no matter how deeply the truth had wounded, he'd been helping. And today, he'd gently helped her remove that ugly hook from a silly little duck, now lovesick over *him.*

Could she blame the bird for preferring him over her? Cole was easygoing, except when he was telling her she was a fool. He seemed content with his life. Jen wished she had the ability to be content with hers. Always driven, striving for perfection, could be wearing.

Jen was looking for a husband with a good education and career goals similar to hers, so why was she so illogically attracted to Cole? Another question bullied its way into her head. Who did Cole have a date with, and would he be back tonight? The fact that those questions tortured her was infuriating, and her defenses went up like a drawbridge. She would not think about it. *She did not care!* She would fix him dinner tomorrow night because she owed him for his help. The meal would be brief, business-like— and if she was very lucky, edible.

The next day progressed like the ones before. Disastrously, or nearly so. Cole was true to his word, and arrived at 8:00 a.m. sharp, with his bare chest, macho attitude and lethal nail gun. At noon, he surprised her by splitting a tuna salad sandwich with her. There was no ceremony about it. She walked into the kitchen to grab some coffee between appointments and he asked if she was hungry. She was starving, and too preoccupied with her worries to deny it, so she nodded. Without further conversation, he slid her his plate containing half of his sandwich. Then he'd left the kitchen to go upstairs to continue whatever he was working on.

Fine! Now she owed him for lunch, too. Well, tonight's dinner would pay her debt in full. Last night she'd driven to Corpus Christi, thirty minutes away along the coast, and bought groceries. She had all the supplies she needed. She'd decided to make one of the two or three meals she could prepare successfully most of the time—a recipe of her mother's she called Roast Pork à la Norma, along with simple baked potatoes and herbed veggie strips. The most complicated thing about this meal was cutting uniform strips of zucchini, carrots and leeks.

She'd done that, with only a few strips that she'd had to toss. The pork was roasting, filling the air with its mouth-watering fragrance. Browned the night before it had been ready to cook. Between appointments she'd removed it from the fridge and popped it in the oven.

Interestingly, as the baking pork's aroma spread through the house, late-afternoon applicants seemed more positive about the marriage idea. That told her the meat was giving them the false subliminal message that she would be the ''little wifey,'' making herself available to fix ''her man's'' dinners. Becoming a short-order cook was *not* part of her game plan. If anything she would like her husband to be able to cook.

Her head snapped up with a thought as she basted the pork with pan juices. Cole could cook. "No, Jen!" She slammed the oven door. "Don't even think it!" She reminded herself that both career-wise and education-wise Cole was not what she had in mind. Which was just as well, since he found her as sexy as a frozen fish.

Though she hadn't actually asked him about his educational background, he couldn't have much schooling to be satisfied with the handyman job. Jen planned to marry a man with excellent credentials, a man with ambition, someone she could point to with pride.

Cole didn't even wear a shirt! Could she take him to formal business dinners? Could he hold up his end of the conversation with movers-and-shakers in the financial world? The notion seemed unimaginable. She squeezed her eyes shut, muttering, "So stop thinking about him!"

Dinner proceeded amid an air of discomfort, at least on Jen's part. Cole seemed at his usual ease, if not particularly cheerful. He had gone so far as to say the meal was good, managing to do it without acting insultingly surprised.

Though he'd made it clear he disapproved of her husband search, he had put his scowls aside for the duration of the meal.

Movement caught her eye and her uneasy glance slid to him as he lifted the tumbler of tea to his lips. She winced at the reminder that she'd forgotten to fix anything to drink. Cole had gone back to his cottage to get the sun tea he'd made that day. She hated to admit it was the best tea she'd ever tasted.

As he drank, Jen began to feel the pressure of the enduring silence. Not that they'd done much talking. Maybe the tension had become unbearable because he'd turned his gaze on her as he drank. She shoved her vegetable strips around on her plate, her stomach tight with tension.

"So—why haven't you done more with your life?" she asked, then flinched. Had she voiced that aloud? She held her breath, focusing on her plate and her hardly touched meal. If he didn't respond, then she hadn't blurted it out. If he did, well, she was no stranger to being on the receiving end of his glower.

Jen poked at a piece of meat with her fork. The pork stuck on the prongs, and she suddenly didn't know what to do. A lump had formed in her throat and she feared if she tried to eat it, she would choke. Flustered, she lay the fork aside, waiting. A few more seconds of silence, and she'd be in the clear.

His tumbler clanked to the tabletop. "Is this a formal interview, Miss Sancroft?" he asked, his tone taunting.

Oh, heavens! She really had asked that out loud! What masochistic imp in her head made that decision? Determined to avoid the sticky truth, she shook her head, passing him her most innocent stare. "Why, no!" she lied. "I—I was simply making dinner conversation."

He peered at her. "No, you weren't. Dinner conversation is 'How was your day?' not 'Why haven't you done more with your life?'"

He had an uncomfortable point, but she forged on with her bluff. "You're free to believe what you want." She took up her fork with its fragment of pork and bit it off, feigning a cool facade. She only hoped, when the time came, she could swallow.

As she chewed, the room returned to a deafening silence. She managed to get the food down, and made herself look at him. To boost her side of the argument and her ego, she told him, "It's not as though I haven't had some excellent results!" Translated, she'd interviewed two men this morning with adequate résumés, who might be interested in, if not overjoyed about, her proposition. "*Several* applicants are *highly* enthusiastic," she lied brightly. "I'm very, very positive about a successful outcome." That was a pretty tall tale, but she couldn't help it. She found it crucial to wipe that skeptical frown off his face.

"Really?" His gaze was steady, probing.

She nodded, but couldn't form words. It had been a mistake to stare directly into those opalescent eyes. She experienced an extraordinary sensual pull that made her heart race and her breath catch. At the same time, she felt an incomprehensible contentment, an unexplainable sense of coming home. Her logical, experienced side screamed, *Beware, Jennifer, it's the Pink Haze Syndrome all over again! Don't weaken because of his seductive eyes!*

With great difficulty she looked away. Staring too long was dangerous—they could hypnotize and bend the mind. Why couldn't she learn that?

With great sorrow, she realized she couldn't remember either of the adequate applicant's names.

She moved through the meal in a daze. Somewhere in her mental fog, she heard Cole speak, and flicked him her reluctant glance. "What?"

He lay his fork aside and Jen noticed his plate was empty. Where had she gone in her head? She shook off the impulse to remember, fairly sure she'd dwelled on the very man she was trying so hard to ignore.

"I said, how about a swim?"

She frowned, confused. "You and me?"

He nodded. "That's the idea."

Was he kidding? "You—and me?" she repeated, looking for a trick.

"It's not rocket science," he said, his attention fixed on her face, as though checking for signs of a stroke. "Just a suggestion."

"But—but we just ate," she said lamely.

He grinned, the show of teeth terribly unfair. Though the smile was more mocking than friendly, it still had a harmful effect on her ability to reason. "If my suggestion included hard swimming, you might need to fear stomach cramps."

He sat back, his gaze challenging. "I'm talking about a romp in the waves."

She stared. *A romp?* The outlandish visions that romped in her mind were breathtakingly erotic—especially considering her lack of experience in that area.

"Scared?" he asked. She wondered if he could read minds. That's exactly what she was. Scared to death. Not so much of him, but of herself, of what she might do during a moonlight swim with Cole Noone. She couldn't form any response.

He lifted a questioning eyebrow. "Come now, Miss Sancroft. If you can't trust your bodyguard, who can you trust?"

His reminder that he found her so unstimulating made her mad. Her ability to speak clicked on. "I'm not afraid," she gritted out, throwing caution to the wind. "I do feel like a—a romp!" Belatedly she remembered she hadn't brought a suit. "Oh…"

"Oh?" he asked.

She shook her head. "I don't have a swimsuit."

He looked surprised. "You're staying at a seaside home without any intention of swimming?"

Her annoyance swelled. She wanted to lie and say her plan was to swim in the nude, but she wouldn't put it past him to badger her into proving it. Instead she shrugged. "You know why I came here, and it wasn't to flounce around in the surf."

"Ah, yes." He stood up. "I seem to remember seeing guest swimsuits in an upstairs closet when I was repairing a shelf." He gave her a once-over, his expression unreadable. "There should be something that would fit you."

She didn't know how to read his look, but considering their recent history, she decided to be insulted. "Fine, I'll look in the *priggish* section."

He pursed his lips, and she sensed he might be masking wry amusement. Well, so what! Why should she care what he thought?

"Good luck with it." He reached for his plate, and she had the feeling he was going to help clear the table.

"Don't!"

He glanced at her, obviously perplexed by her vehemence.

She stood and stepped around the corner of the table to grab his plate. "This was an appreciation dinner for your help. You go on—start romping."

Without responding he stepped back to give her room as she busied herself gathering his silverware. Why must she be so aware of his nearness?

"Actually, I was planning to get seconds," he said, startling her so badly she almost dropped his plate.

"You were what?" She faced him.

He removed his plate and silverware from her hands and returned the utensils to the table. "Seconds," he repeated. "You know, after the first, but before the third?" Indicating the kitchen with the plate, he added, "If you don't mind? The pork is delicious."

"Uh—why, no. I guess not..."

"Thanks." He stepped around her and walked into the kitchen. She glanced down at his silverware. "Seconds?" Had he actually said the pork was delicious? In a state of awe, she gaped at the dining room door through which he'd disappeared. Strangely weak, she rested her palms on the cool, glass tabletop. After a moment, she heard singing filter through the stereo sound system. She didn't recognize the music, something operatic in a foreign language.

Cole reappeared in the doorway, his plate piled with pork as well as the last of the vegetables. He set his food on the table then glanced at her. "Am I in your way?"

She blinked, realizing she was leaning on the table next to his chair. She straightened. "No—no." Befuddled, she returned to her place and was disconcerted further when he held her chair for her as she sat down.

"I hope you don't mind my turning on the music," he said as he took his seat. "I enjoy French arias."

She glanced at him, startled by the remark. "That's a French aria?"

"One of the best in my opinion, Dominique's farewell to the forests from *L'attaque du moulin.*"

"Oh," she said, not quite sure how to respond, since she had no experience with arias, French or otherwise. "I see." That seemed generic enough not to sound totally clueless. "Is that a compact disk?"

He nodded. "Mine. I brought several over before you arrived, to listen to while I work. But with the interviews going on..." His shrug took the statement to its obvious conclusion.

"Oh." What else could she say? "Well, it's—interesting."

"You don't like it?"

She sat back and took a deep breath, trying to appear conversational though her heart raced unmercifully. "Why would you say that?"

"Because you used the word 'interesting,' as in the ancient Chinese curse, 'May you live in interesting times.'"

She blanched at his hypothesis. She hadn't put as much thought into her remark as he apparently had. "I didn't mean it that way. I think it's very nice."

"Are you familiar with it?"

She cleared her throat. "Well—I know French is a language spoken in France and an aria is an operatic solo."

His smile seemed almost genuine, with just a touch of mockery around the edges. "Very good, Miss Sancroft."

Though she hardly needed to admit her ignorance, she somehow couldn't help herself. "My knowledge of this particular aria *might* have a few, tiny gaps."

"Well, to fill the gaps, it's based on Zola's tale. In this scene, a Flemish soldier has been captured by the Germans and condemned to death for aiding their French enemies. As he waits for his execution at dawn, he sings goodbye to the trees and the sky. The artist, Cordule Poirier, with his magnificent baritone voice, makes it an extraordinary moment. Listen.''

Jen concentrated on the solo with all her might, picturing a doomed soldier singing out his heart on the eve before he is to die. How beautiful, how stirring it was, especially now that she knew the story. ''I like it,'' she said, aware her comment was inadequate in light of the utter beauty of the piece. She knew a lot about finances, politics and current events, but practically nothing about music.

Feeling uncharacteristically exposed and vulnerable, she shifted her attention to his face. ''How—how did you get interested in French arias?''

He held her gaze, his pitifully willing prisoner. Laying aside his fork, he said, ''What you mean is, how could a handyman know about opera?''

She experienced a prick at his shrewd comment. ''You think I'm a terrible snob, don't you?''

He pursed his lips, his silence a tacit rebuke.

''I'd rather think we have very different outlooks,'' she murmured, dropping her gaze to her plate.

''No argument there.''

She flicked him a wary look. Dark, glossy hair, attractively windblown from his trek across the lawn gave him just the right touch of masculine charm. His pristine-white polo shirt fitted nicely across broad shoulders and proved once and for all that he actually did own a shirt—and he could look every bit as sexy wearing one as not.

Beneath the glass tabletop she could see his unbleached canvas trousers, clean and pressed and in no way disguising the power and span of his long legs. His tan, leather loafers were buffed and unscuffed. Shifting her gaze to his face, she was struck again by his light blue eyes, so direct and intent, too striking to stare into for very long and hold on to her good judgment.

She looked away. She must sort out her thoughts, arrange them, impose order. Okay, maybe he *could* wear a shirt when it was called for, and he knew more about French arias than she did. Even so, he wasn't the upwardly mobile kind of guy she was looking for. That wasn't being snobbish, it was just being logical. Wasn't it?

The aria faded and he sat back. "That was great. Thank you."

She wasn't positive he was referring to the dinner and not the aria, but he had complimented her on the meal and he'd eaten a lot of food, so she nodded, working on a pleasant expression. He'd been a perfectly polite guest, even if his compliment had been surrounded by comments that made her feel dumb and guilty. "It was nothing. I owed you this dinner," she said, making herself look at him. She picked up her tumbler to take a sip.

"I'll go change."

She peered at him over her glass. Change? What was he talking about?

Her confusion must have been apparent on her face, since he added, "Remember?" He stood up. "I suggested a swim?"

She replaced her tumbler with a clank. "Oh—right." *The romp*. On second thought, she wasn't sure agreeing to that had been a good idea. "Actually, Cole—"

"I'll go change," he cut in. Gripping the back of his chair, he leaned toward her. "You weren't thinking of backing out were you?"

She didn't like the implication that he thought she was a chicken. She decided to lie. "No, it's not that—"

"Good. I'll see you in half an hour on the beach." She started to stand, to take her argument to the door, but he motioned her to remain seated. "I can see myself out."

"But…" In three strides he reached the front door. A moment later it clicked shut, and he was gone. She curled her hands around the edge of the tabletop. Dinner with Cole had caused her more emotional turbulence than the toughest IRS audit she'd ever endured. And somewhere in all that turbulence she'd actually agreed to *romp* in the surf with him! "Was I insane?" she asked in a forlorn whisper.

Fifteen minutes later, Jen stared at herself in the mirrored wall over the master bathroom's tub. From all the new swimsuits available, she'd actually chosen a hot pink, two piece. *Face it, Jen,* she insisted silently. *It's not just a two-piece, it's a bikini!* She'd never paraded around in so little clothing except during a physical exam. And Cole Noone was no medical doctor. What was going on with her? What had happened to her celebrated logic, her convictions gleaned from hard-fought experience, her grim vow to steer clear of Cole Noone and his hypnotic eyes?

She was afraid she knew. Cole had made it so clear how blasé he felt about her, he'd bloodied her pride. She frowned at herself, hiking up the skimpy bodice. Fidgety fingers adjusted the straps that rose from between her breasts, then retied them behind her neck. Hitching up the thin ribbon of fabric at one hip, she endured a twinge of self-doubt. "Maybe the black, one-piece would be wiser."

As she grabbed a towel and left her bathroom to dash down the stairs, her mind shouted, *The black one-piece would be much wiser!*

Sadly, Jen wasn't into wisdom at the moment; she was into wounded pride.

CHAPTER SIX

AT THE back door Jen wrapped the towel around her shoulders like a shawl, second thoughts about her rash choice in swimming attire gnawing at her. What did she think she was doing? She turned around, absolutely sure the black one-piece was the swimsuit she should wear.

After only two steps she forced herself to stop, to settle down and think. She had put on that pink bikini for a reason. That know-it-all handyman who'd taunted her to *romp* with him in the surf had scolded and mocked her for the past week. He'd called her priggish—and a virgin, like it was some huge flaw. He'd made it clear she was as sexless as the tax code. He'd actually told her she would be no strain to protect against attackers.

Well, she might not be a voluptuous sexpot, but she was a woman. A woman in search of a spouse. Cole's snipes at her femininity had put a dent in her self-confidence. She was tired of being glared at with arrogant disapproval. She was fed up with continued remarks about her selfishness and the stupidity of her efforts. Her motives were far less self-serving than he insisted on believing. She was sincerely looking for a life partner, someone she could make a home with, someone she could learn to care for and have children with.

She couldn't do much about his negative assumptions about her spouse hunt, but tonight was her chance to punch a hole in his attitude about her lack of sex appeal. She wasn't forgetting about her promise to herself after Tony. She was correct in her decision *not* to dress like a mantrap, because going after a man that way got you only the most superficial men.

But she wasn't interested in "trapping" Cole Noone. She just wanted to—to unsettle *him,* for a change. Call it a test case. She would prove to the troublesome Mr. Noone that she was every inch a woman. She simply wasn't in the market for a man with so little depth he couldn't appreciate her on an intellectual level. To put it bluntly, tonight, in her little pink bikini, she planned to turn Cole Noone on and then walk away victorious.

Drawing a deep breath, she dragged the towel from about her shoulders. "Okay, Cole," she muttered, yanking open the back door. "Let's romp!"

Cole stood in the surf, staring up at the cloudless night. Scattered across the inky sky an abundance of stars flickered and blinked like far-off flashbulbs, as though struggling to compete with the huge, golden moon. He sucked in a breath of briny air, annoyed with himself. What had caused him to taunt Miss Priss into a *romp,* whatever the hell that meant? No matter how he ran it through his mind, it had a clear-cut sexual implication, which was a complete about-face of anything he'd meant to suggest.

He closed his eyes and grimaced at the memory of his needling. *If you can't trust your bodyguard, who can you trust?*

Good question. That quip was a blast of swagger he wasn't sure he believed. Who could she really trust? He muttered a self-directed oath, telling himself the answer to that question had better be *him.*

In the past thirty minutes, he'd decided that rather than hold that dinner meeting for the first D.A.A. presidential candidate and his wife last night, as he had, he should have really had a date. He should have taken his private jet someplace more exotic and romantic than Dallas, should have met some willing female for a romp of an entirely different kind from the one he was regretting he'd invited Miss Priss to join him in tonight. He needed a woman. How else could he explain such an absurd invitation?

"She won't show up," he muttered, not sure how he would feel if she didn't. Relieved? Infuriated? Rejected?

A door slammed, and he grew alert. Maybe he was wrong. It sounded like she was coming after all. His gut tightened, and once again he asked himself why—why had he made the idiotic invitation?

He felt out of sync, mentally divided. He wondered if she had put on a swimsuit, or if she'd chickened out and planned to tell him to start without her. *Start without her.* He flinched at the sexual connotation. *Get off it, Barringer,* he commanded silently. *You don't like her self-centered scheme to get ahead, so don't let your lack of sex lately make you do something stupid.*

Shifting toward the house he saw movement as she emerged from the blackness of the covered deck and came down the steps to the lawn. The full moon and clear night made her easy to see—her anatomy showcased in the moonlight.

One thing was positive. She had not chickened out. It was obvious she wore little—or nothing. He watched her approach in open shock so acute he was no longer sure of his reason. Was she even wearing a suit? Surely she was. In the false light of night, it was hard to tell from a distance. Common sense told him she had to be wearing something. He couldn't have miscalculated that completely.

The sight of her moving across the lawn, shoulders high as she dragged a towel in her wake, sent a shudder of lust rampaging through him. "Damn," he muttered, wondering if he could be trusted to keep his hands off her. From what he could see, she was equipped with an abundance of feminine attributes. If she'd been interviewing all week in the buff, she'd have a panting, drooling list of ready candidates standing in line to be her husband.

He heard a bang, and became aware that she'd closed the gate and was approaching over the grassy dunes. When she'd come within twenty paces of him, he could tell she had on some kind of swimsuit, though far skimpier than anything he imagined she would choose.

She stepped onto the sand, chin high. Her towel dangled from one hand, trawling the sand in a serpentine trail, the act highly erotic.

She walked toward him, her long, shapely legs tempting mutely. Slender waist, teasing navel and barely contained breasts, quivering seductively with every step, made his stomach clench with raw desire. He gritted his teeth to keep the pain of her hip-swaying advance from showing on his face.

She came to a stop just out of reach—a wise decision— and lifted her chin a notch higher, the queen of defiance. He couldn't suppress a spark of admiration, but masked it with a cynical look. "Couldn't find the priggish section?" he asked, keeping his tone careless.

"I found it." She let the towel drop to the sand and placed her hands on her hips. "I ignored it."

"That's obvious." He had an urge to smile at her defiant spirit, but resisted. If she knew the sexy images running around in his brain, she'd be heading, screaming toward the house. Unfortunately, as her blasted bodyguard, he couldn't initiate any of the things he was thinking. "What made you do that?"

With a slight smile of challenge, she tossed her head. "I work in an accounting firm, I don't swim in one."

"Apparently you don't."

Could he actually feel the heat of her skin from that distance? So *much* skin, too. Hot desire shot through him, and the night breeze told him beads of sweat had formed on his forehead.

"Okay, you're the romp expert," she said. "What happens now?" She clasped her hands behind her. The move served to thrust her breasts toward him. He winced at the fire in his gut, wondering if she'd done that on purpose.

The silence stretched on for a starlit eternity.

"Well?" she repeated. "I'm here, ready to romp."

He glowered at her, an urge to grab her and drag her down into the sand, make wild love to her, warred with his dislike for everything she represented. Before he lost his mind completely, he needed distance from the curvy, near-naked little siren. "I've changed my mind, Miss Sancroft." His voice was gruffer than he would have liked. "I think I'll take a swim—alone." Translation—your bodyguard seems to have developed an irrational case of the hots for you. Before I do something I'll regret, I'm putting distance—and cold water—between us.

Deeply troubled and angry with himself, he turned his back and ran into the surf, his shallow dive slicing through the waves. With every ounce of determination and strength he could marshal, he swam away.

Jen didn't know how long it took her to absorb the fact that Cole had abandoned her *and* her pink bikini there on the beach. The world had become quiet, but for the boom of the surf as it rushed in, again and again and again. At some point, she found herself sitting, burrowing her fingers in the sand. *Could she be more demoralized?*

She had a husband to acquire, hopefully a nice, safe, prosperous man she could learn to love. How could she continue in her search if she allowed herself to believe Cole's indifference was typical, a harsh exercise in how hopelessly unappealing she was? Had Tony been so depraved he was willing to seduce even the least appealing woman on earth? Had she deluded herself into thinking she'd ever had any sex appeal? She squeezed her eyes shut, fisting her hands in the sand.

No! That was a horrible thought. She groaned, too depressed to cry. After a while, around the corner of her mind, a thought began to form. Why was she allowing this handyman to hold such power over her self-confidence? He had no ambition. No position. She fisted her hands in the sand, telling herself to snap out of this fixation on a man who was no more right for her than—than the infatuated mallard that had flown after him as he dived into the sea.

"Stupid, smitten bird," she muttered. Angry with herself for letting Cole make her doubt herself, she shoved herself up from the sand. Spinning in the direction of the house, she collided with a big, solid male.

"*Oh!*" she cried, stumbling backward. Before she could fall, somebody caught her upper arms, steadying her.

Her fight-or-flight instinct took over and she yanked to free herself, run for her life, but she couldn't break away. She opened her mouth to scream, at that instant registering that the interloper who held her captive was the very man who tormented her thoughts.

"You!" she cried. "How—how did you…" She shook her head, trying to make sense of the fact that Cole was no longer swimming madly away, but standing there holding her prisoner. His hair, face, torso, glistened with water, highlighting his strong features and muscular build. Her mind cried out, *How dare you be so breathtaking in the moonlight!*

His jaw bunched in what had to be annoyance. She decided to take the offensive, beat him to the punch for once. "What do you think you're doing?" she demanded.

"Getting run into," he muttered.

"I thought you were swimming."

"I was." He watched her with inscrutable, steely eyes. "I'm not now." His tone grew chillier by the second, his words beginning to bite.

Her heart hammered, thundering in her ears. Desperate to appear as impatient and severe as he, she willed herself to turn to stone. "Well—that's obvi—"

His lips claimed hers and he crushed her to him. His mouth, warm, moist and persuasive, left her lips burning, her brain on fire. After a few heartbeats, her initial shock gave way, his kiss sparking an answering response deep inside her. A golden wave of passion surged upward, outward from her core, and on their own her arms encircled his neck. The texture of his skin, his hair was divine under her hands, and she reveled in the feel.

The concave hollow of her spine tingled with the contact of his fingers, spreading across her skin, kneading, heating, seducing. She became aware of his arousal, thrust hard against her, and some unruly part of her thrilled.

She pressed wantonly into him, her kiss deepening, making her responding desire clear. Her lips parted and he accepted her offer, his tongue at first making feather-light love to the inner recesses of her mouth, then smoldering, urging, dazzling, all-consuming mastery she knew would bring her wild, sweet release.

Passion pounded the blood through her heart, head, chest. Her whole body was aflame; her impatience for him grew to explosive proportions. These sensations were new, unprecedented, but so right. She breathed in deep, soul-drenching drafts, savoring his scent, mingled with the tang of the sea. A tantalizing combination, it made her dizzy with longing. The world careened and she clung to him to keep from falling. Her defenses were deliriously gone, a casualty of his bold touch and electrifying kisses.

She was his for the taking.

His mouth lifted away from hers and grazed her earlobe. He whispered something against her temple, but she couldn't comprehend the words.

"Hmm?" she asked dreamily, holding him, clinging, limp and willing.

His hands slid from her back, jarring her when they gripped her upper arms. Startled and confused, she opened her eyes.

"I said," he muttered huskily, "before you *interview* the finalists—your kiss needs work."

CHAPTER SEVEN

COLE sat at the kitchen table in his two-room cabin, staring into his half-empty coffee mug. He couldn't get his mind off last night and his crazy behavior. What had made him go back to that beach? Why had he grabbed Jen and kissed her? The memory caused renewed hunger to come on in a heated rush. He slammed his mug down, quelling the unwanted feelings.

He'd been unable to sleep all night, damning himself and wondering why in blazes he'd said Jen's kiss needed work. The truth was her kisses were so blasted awesome she could lecture on the subject! Guilt stomped through his consciousness. He'd spent hours beating himself up, speculating on why he'd growled such a bold-faced lie. Somewhere around dawn it came to him. It had been a stab at self-preservation, a tactless attempt to put distance between himself and a scheming woman he felt an unexplainable attraction for.

He'd kissed her, conscious only of her nearness, her lips—lips sending fire through every nerve in his body— then he'd had a fleeting memory of his father's hopeless love for his mother. It had been in that instant that he'd snarled the rejection.

His withdrawal had come too late to allow him to walk away unscathed. He felt like a shipwrecked seafarer. No woman's kiss had affected him that way. Hell, no woman's kiss had affected him at all—except for momentary gratification.

Why did Jennifer Sancroft's taste linger? The memory of fireworks exploding in his brain during the encounter

PLAY

LUCKY HEARTS

GAME

AND YOU GET

- **FREE BOOKS!**
- **A FREE GIFT!**
- **YOURS TO KEEP!**

TURN THE PAGE AND DEAL YOURSELF IN...

Play **LUCKY HEARTS** for this..

exciting FREE gift!
This surprise mystery gift could be yours free

when you play **LUCKY HEARTS!**
...then continue your lucky streak with a sweetheart of a deal!

1. Play Lucky Hearts as instructed on the opposite page.

2. Send back this card and you'll receive 2 brand-new Harlequin Romance® books. These books have a cover price of $3.99 each in the U.S., and $4.50 each in Canada, but they are yours to keep absolutely free.

3. There's no catch! You're under no obligation to buy anything. We charge nothing— ZERO—for your first shipment. And you don't have to make any minimum number of purchases—not even one!

4. The fact is thousands of readers enjoy receiving their books by mail from the Harlequin Reader Service®. They enjoy the convenience of home delivery...they like getting the best new novels at discount prices, BEFORE they're available in stores...and they love their *Heart to Heart* subscriber newsletter featuring author news, horoscopes, recipes, book reviews and much more!

5. We hope that after receiving your free books you'll want to remain a subscriber. But the choice is yours—to continue or cancel, any time at all! So why not take us up on our invitation, with no risk of any kind. You'll be glad you did!

Visit us online at

www.eHarlequin.com

- **Exciting Harlequin® romance books— FREE!**
- **Plus an exciting mystery gift—FREE!**
- **No cost! No obligation to buy!**

YES!

I have scratched off the silver card. Please send me the 2 FREE books and gift for which I qualify.
I understand I am under no obligation to purchase any books, as explained on the back and on the opposite page.

With a coin, scratch off the silver card and check below to see what we have for you.

LUCKY HEARTS GAME

386 HDL DRPC   **186 HDL DRPT**

FIRST NAME	LAST NAME

ADDRESS

APT.#	CITY

STATE/PROV.   ZIP/POSTAL CODE

Twenty-one gets you 2 free books, and a free mystery gift!

Twenty gets you 2 free books!

Nineteen gets you 1 free book!

Try Again!

Offer limited to one per household and not valid to current Harlequin Romance® subscribers. All orders subject to approval.

(H-R-11/02)

The Harlequin Reader Service®—Here's how it works:

Accepting your 2 free books and gift places you under no obligation to buy anything. You may keep the books and gift and return the shipping statement marked "cancel." If you do not cancel, about a month later we'll send you 6 additional books and bill you just $3.34 each in the U.S., or $3.80 each in Canada, plus 25¢ shipping & handling per book and applicable taxes if any.* That's the complete price and — compared to cover prices of $3.99 each in the U.S. and $4.50 each in Canada — it's quite a bargain! You may cancel at any time, but if you choose to continue, every month we'll send you 6 more books, which you may either purchase at the discount price or return to us and cancel your subscription.

*Terms and prices subject to change without notice. Sales tax applicable in N.Y. Canadian residents will be charged applicable provincial taxes and GST.

refused to fade. Why had he reacted so intensely to a mere meeting of lips? It was a troubling mystery.

To get his mind off the kiss of a woman he shouldn't find attractive, he'd pulled out his laptop computer, deciding to work on analysis charts for the three vice presidents vying for the D.A.A. president slot. He'd finished the one for Melvin Seals, the vice president he'd dined with on Thursday evening. A good man. Steady. Intelligent. Humorless.

Working at his kitchen table, he'd begun the chart for Jennifer Sancroft. So far, under "possible problems" he'd written, "too methodical," "does not trust her instincts" and "no passion."

No passion? After that kiss?

He ground out an oath. *Shut up about the kiss, Barringer!* He took a sip of cold coffee and grimaced, then typed in, "overly career-oriented."

Was that really a negative? Would he have written that about Melvin if he were single? Melvin had a wife to care for their three children while Melvin did his forty to sixty hours a week and traveled to meetings or seminars.

He deleted that and typed, "cares deeply for animals." It had nothing to do with her job and wasn't even in the right column, but the recollection of her standing on the beach, clutching that squirming duck, made him smile. She'd been so frightened, but absolutely determined to help. That showed courage. Essential in a good leader.

"Makes a great roast pork." Maybe she didn't admit to being a cook, and maybe she didn't cook very much, but what she did cook, she cooked well. She was clearly a perfectionist and didn't give herself *any* credit for things she didn't do perfectly. Was that a flaw? Should that be put in the negative column or the positive column? Wasn't he a perfectionist in a lot of ways?

"Cute little wiggle." He lounged back in his chair, staring at the words he'd just typed. "What in the *hell?*" Angry with himself for the bizarre and unprofessional notation, he deleted it. So she swayed a little when she walked; so it had been more obvious when she'd worn that bikini. It did *not* belong in her analysis chart. Was he losing his mind?

He cleared his throat and told himself to get back to business. He was assessing positive and negative traits, not composing a valentine! "Nice smile," he typed.

"Damn!" He deleted the assessment, wondering what was the matter with him today. Was his lack of sex lately coupled with the unexpected sensuality of her kiss turning his brain to mush?

It damn well better not be love, a voice in his head warned. *Love?* Where had that notion come from? What he was feeling couldn't be love. He had no intention of giving away his heart to some self-serving, calculating female.

If Miss Sancroft had any idea he was the "old coot J. C. Barringer," she would be purring in his lap right now. He knew how women like her operated. Though the notion of her cuddled in his lap set off an uninvited sizzle in his belly, he had no intention of playing a repeat performance of his father's mistake. Not bloody likely!

A banging at his door brought his head up with a snap. He checked his wristwatch. Eight o'clock. On a Saturday morning? "Just a second," he called, his annoyance over his troubled thoughts evident in his shout. He shook his head, trying to shed his bad humor. Jennifer Sancroft didn't deserve that much of his mental energy. "Who is it?"

"It's me," came the response, sounding far from thrilled to be there.

He frowned, staring at his door as though it had become radioactive. After a second's hesitation, he snapped his laptop closed and covered it with his newspaper. He got up, his chair scraping along pine planks. Crossing the room, he swung the door wide.

There she stood, obviously frazzled. Brushing her hair with one hand, she fumbled to fasten her top shirt button with the other. "I'm in a jam," she said, looking distraught.

"Apparently Ruthie made an appointment for today. A guy just showed up. I was in my robe! I made an excuse to run over here and—and—and I need to hold the interview, but—but I'd rather not do it alone." She took a hard swipe at her hair and lost her grip on the brush. It clattered to the porch.

She bent to retrieve it, but Cole beat her to it. They straightened in unison, and he handed it back to her. "Thanks," she mumbled, not meeting his eyes.

He could tell she was having a rough time looking at him. So far she'd looked almost everywhere but at his face. Could he blame her? As much as his disparaging remark about her kiss haunted him, it must have really skewered her. He owed her an apology.

"I've got to get back," she said. "Will you help me—or not?"

Feeling like a jerk, he nodded. "Of course. I'll get my tools."

The flash of relief that crossed her features affected him more than it should have. "Thanks," she repeated, finally meeting his eyes. But the contact was brief. She turned away, headed across the porch and opened the screened door. Hesitating, she looked back. "You realize I wouldn't ask if there was any other way."

He shrugged his hands into his hip pockets. "Look, Jen," he said, needing to make amends. "I'm sorry for that remark about—"

"You have a right to your opinion," she cut in. The anguish glimmering in her eyes made him feel like he'd swallowed ground glass.

"Yes, but—"

The bang of the screened door and the sight of her dashing off, told him she had no plans to discuss it. Jennifer Sancroft was a frustrating and unique experience.

With a muffled oath, he turned away to get his tools.

Jen took a last swipe at her hair, tossed the brush on the den sofa and dashed into the living room to rejoin the unexpected applicant. "Well, Mr. McDermott, I'm sorry about the confusion. You see my assistant had to leave suddenly, and I wasn't aware she'd scheduled appointments for the weekend."

"It's McDonnett. Kevin McDonnett," he said, looking over his shoulder from his seat on the sofa. He didn't smile, typical for job applicants, usually nervous and self-conscious. Somehow his discomfort gave her confidence. That was the whole point of this husband hunt, to control her destiny.

She put on her business face. "Mr. McDonnett, of course." She took a seat on one of two wing chairs, trying to get her mind off Cole. Dwelling on last night's humbling experience couldn't do anything but erode her poise. Yet, even as she began the interview, asking well-worn questions, her mind seemed unable to solidly connect with the responses.

She was reluctantly beginning to face the fact that what she wanted in a husband wasn't what she needed. As Cole had warned, the most successful of the men would want nothing to do with her marriage plan. Only those less driven, less successful had been interested, so far. Those men, she found, she didn't have much respect for.

She feared compromises might have to be made. Her standards may have to be altered. Still, she held out a desperate hope that between now and Tuesday evening, the last day she'd set aside for preliminary interviews, she would find someone—preferably three adequate and willing "someones"—who would become finalists. On Wednesday, Thursday and Friday of next week she would conduct in-depth interviews involving one finalist per day, and ultimately secure a satisfactory husband.

"Yes, I suppose I'd be interested," Mr. McDonnett said, startling Jen from her musings. "I've been thinking of settling down."

"Pardon?" In the middle of a distracted doodle on her

notepad, Jen looked up. At first, her mind was blank, refusing to grasp the statement. In his brown eyes she was stunned to see a degree of interest she was not accustomed to receiving from applicants. Her emotions did a quick roller coaster dip and rise, dip and rise, making her feel what she could only describe as motion sickness. She swallowed hard.

The front door opened and Jen's attention moved on its own to gaze at Cole as he came inside and shut the door behind him. Shirtless, a tool belt about his waist, every move causing the metal accoutrements to clank in a machomanly way. His gaze rested briefly on her and she felt the heat of it before he turned his attention to her companion. "Sorry for the intrusion," he said, his voice booming.

Mr. McDonnett shifted to stare at Cole over his shoulder, cleared his throat and stiffened noticeably. Jen was so stung, so hurt, from last night's encounter, she wanted to hate Cole. Too bad that once he walked in, she found herself having difficulty catching her breath. The thick tension in the air made her woozy. All she could do was sit there, woodenly, unfocused, suffering shortness of breath as she struggled to remain outwardly unmoved.

"Who—who's that?" McDonnett asked. The anxiousness in his voice jogged her from her daze. "Don't worry, Kevin," she said, a slight tremor in her voice. "It's only my handyman." With a reluctant glance toward Cole, she added, "Go ahead, Mr. Noone. You won't disturb us." She only wished that were true. He was so disturbing even his cruel remark last night hadn't dulled his charisma.

"Yes, ma'am." He nodded. When Kevin turned back to look worriedly at Cole, he wordlessly threatened him with bodily harm if he even looked at her funny. "Howdy, friend," he drawled, stone-faced.

"Uh—hello…" Kevin said.

With another grim nod, Cole tromped and clanked toward the back of the house. "If you need me, Miss Sancroft, just shout," he added, his meaning loud and clear.

When Kevin faced her again, he looked tense. Cole's Me-Tarzan charade had once again done its job. He might find her totally unappetizing, but she had to give him credit. He was giving his bodyguard act his best efforts. If he ratcheted his performance one notch higher he'd have her applicants running for their lives.

Feeling more secure from Cole's playacting, she recrossed her legs and focused on her companion. "Forgive the interruption, but I'm a person who believes in conscientious time management. If a thing needs doing, I don't believe in putting it off, even if it causes a little inconvenience."

McDonnett nodded, looking a little less intimidated now that Cole was no longer towering over him. "I agree." Leaning forward and resting his hands on his knees, he began to talk about his job as manager of the Discount City Superstore in Dallas. Jen heard snatches of it—words like "micro-marketing" and "seasonal and demographic needs."

She feared her attention had wandered, since what he said didn't seem to have much to do with time management. To be safe, she nodded and smiled. "That's very interesting," she said, unhappy to recall what Cole had said about the word "interesting" and its use as a Chinese curse. She shook off the memory and tried to concentrate. "Tell me about yourself, Kevin. Hobbies, that sort of thing," she said, striving to keep her mind on the candidate. After all, he was still sitting there, acting interested.

He wasn't bad-looking, tall, wiry, with a durably boyish face and a head of wavy brown hair. His nose was thin, his nostrils delicate. His smile was pleasant though restrained and unmirthful, probably due to his anxiousness. She took pity on him and tried to find him engaging.

As he talked about himself, she scanned his clothes. He wore a plum-colored, double-breasted suit, baby-blue striped shirt and a navy-and-white checked tie. A little extreme for her taste, but she felt sure he was right in style.

He was still speaking when the doorbell rang. Another

one? Jen exhaled despondently. She feared Ruthie had scheduled meetings all day. Offering Kevin her hand, she asked if he would be willing to return for a more detailed interview next Wednesday.

When he agreed, they stood and she walked him to the door, jotting down the time and explaining his "finalist" meeting could take most of the day.

As he left, Jen welcomed in Saturday's applicant number two. She worked at being upbeat. At least she had one finalist, though in her heart she wasn't exactly rejoicing. Nevertheless, Kevin McDonnett had a college degree, managed a large discount store, could speak intelligently, dressed well, wanted to settle down, have children, and he didn't have a problem with a wife as the principal breadwinner. He had so much positive going for him.

It was a shame she felt absolutely no attraction to the man.

At five o'clock the Saturday interviews finally ended. Hurtling closer and closer toward her deadline, Jen was restless and unfocused. Her first applicant, Kevin McDonnett, had been the only tolerable choice all day. For some reason, the fact that she'd actually managed to find a finalist gave her no particular gratification.

Shortly after the last job-seeker drove off, Cole left the house. Jen watched him go, feeling a blurry mix of relief and gloom she didn't care to analyze. Tired and dejected, she slapped together a leftover pork sandwich. Standing at the kitchen counter she ate with little interest. Absently she noticed the French aria compact disk laying on the counter in front of the built-in sound system. For no explainable reason, she slipped it in the player and turned it on.

As she finished off her sandwich an operatic solo filled the stillness. Listless and weary, she stuck her plate and milk glass in the dishwasher. Trudging upstairs to bathe and fall into bed, she held out little hope her sleep would be restful, her dreams, placid. Her nights had become tortured affairs as she tossed and turned, her brain crowded with hot and heady images of the man who thought her kiss needed work.

The compact disk ended then began again, apparently she'd somehow set it on repeat. As she feared, she could find no peace in sleep, the haunting operatic baritone playing again and again, painfully reminiscent of Cole's voice. *Why couldn't she bring herself to turn it off?*

Sunday after breakfast, exhausted and bleary-eyed, she went over her notes from the past week, hoping against hope she'd missed an applicant who may be both satisfactory and willing to get married. After a couple of hours of poring over her meticulously detailed information, she had to admit no one came to light that she'd overlooked.

Tossing the disappointing data in her briefcase, she decided she needed a break. Maybe a swim. Even sunbathe! She must relax, immerse herself in restorative activities. She still had two full days of interviews. She needed to be sharp, rested and focused.

"Give me some choices!" she muttered to the heavens. Yesterday Kevin McDonnett seemed like a good finalist candidate, but right now the idea of marrying him was as thrilling as the prospect of balancing her checkbook. She hoped it was merely a reaction to her fatigue.

Making her decision, she slipped on the pink bikini, silently daring Cole to make a comment. "Let him!" she muttered. "I will ignore him *and* his opinions!"

She found a large, shocking pink beach towel, just the thing for sunbathing on the beach. If Cole was outside, he could hardly miss the neon-pink color. "So what!" she said aloud. "I will not let him have control over my emotions!"

She pranced outside and down the steps, shoulders back, head high. She wanted Cole to read in her posture that she was not cowed by his attitude. If he chided her on the folly of her plan, she could truthfully say she had found a finalist. She was more positive about Kevin now. It was amazing how perspective changed once the big obstacles were overcome.

And Cole had been a *big* obstacle, physically and emotionally. No longer. Her defenses were up and strong. He would not make her doubt herself, ever again. She tried to locate him out of the corner of her eye, but she didn't see him. All the better. She headed toward the gate, bent on soaking up the rays, relax, nourish her spirit.

Sometime later, Jen lay on her stomach, baking in the sunshine. Eyes closed, she listened to the surf, feeling drowsy. Was it any wonder? She'd slept only fitfully since she'd arrived over a week ago. And whose fault was that? She buried her face in the crook of an arm, working to get her mind off Cole and onto the pleasant sunshine and the rush of surf.

She heard a quack, and started, surprised to discover she must have fallen asleep.

"Sorry."

She recognized the masculine voice. By its location, she knew Cole was standing over her. His brief, quiet apology confused her. "What for?" She turned to squint up at him.

"The duck woke you. I saw you jump."

She stared, unsettled by the sight. He wore even less than usual, a pair of dripping black swim trunks that clung in all the right places. Or the wrong places, depending on one's frame of mind. Though she agreed with "right" she needed to go with "wrong." His skin glistened, highlighting every delicious bulge and angle, a troubling vision to deal with in a composed way.

Her heart rate accelerated, making her angry with herself for reacting to him. In self-defense, she closed her eyes and turned to face the sea. "If you and your duck go away, I can go back to sleep."

"Are you wearing sunblock?"

She heaved a sigh. "Of course. No matter what you think, I'm not an idiot."

"You have very fair skin. Be careful."

"Thanks, Mother." Another sharp quack split the air. "I was not speaking to you, duck!" she said. "I was speaking to the big, annoying goose."

She heard a deep, wry chuckle. "If you're referring to me, you should have said gander. Goose is feminine."

Unable to help herself, she turned to face him, rising on one elbow. That gander thing was the last straw. She was through putting up with being told she was wrong by this man. "Go away," she gritted out. "Go away, now!"

Any amusement he might have felt disappeared from his expression. "You should let me put more block on your back."

She heaved an exasperated sigh. "If my back was going up in flames I wouldn't let you hose me down. Is that clear enough?"

"It's pretty clear."

He didn't make any move to leave.

"Don't you have work to do?" she prodded.

"I'm taking the day off."

"Take it off someplace else." Her voice had risen an octave, and she was horrified to discover she was letting him get to her again. Why couldn't she hold on to her composure around this man?

He shrugged, his gaze intent. "Yesterday was supposed to be a day off, too."

She experienced a stab of guilt. "What do you get paid per day? I'll compensate you for yesterday."

He placed his hands on his hips, a treacherous move, at least for her peace of mind. Muscle bunched in his arms and chest, seawater shimmered, emphasizing masculine contours. He looked like one of those power defender toys, only life-size. *Power Beach Bum,* she jeered inwardly, trying to discredit him in her mind. It didn't work.

"I don't want your money, Miss Sancroft."

What do you want, then, to drive me to distraction? she cried mentally, but stopped short of demanding aloud.

"What do you want, then?" she asked, experiencing a flash of discomfort at the sexual implication.

Something stirred in his eyes, but was too quickly gone to reveal what it meant. "I don't want a thing from you," he ground out. "Not a blasted thing."

"I think you do," she retorted, fighting his erotic effect. "I think you want to kill my self-confidence!"

He frowned, actually appearing astonished. *Ha!*

"Well, you're not going to, buster! For your information, my first applicant on Saturday is now a finalist! A perfectly fantastic man. Not only that, I expect to find at least one, probably *two* more, before Wednesday." She sat up, squaring her shoulders. "What do you have to say about that?"

He peered at her, seeming to ponder her statement. After a stressful moment, he said, "Considering a fool is born every minute, I'd say three fools—rather finalists—is certainly feasible." As he finished, he strolled into the water.

Shocked by the quiet put-down, she gasped and twisted to glare after him. "Your insults do *not* bother me!" she shouted, as he dived into the waves. "Don't you walk away from me when I'm talking to you!" she ordered, but he was under water, well out of range.

The duck waddled to the edge of the surf, squawked, flapped her wings and took to the air after him. "Silly bird, how can you stand to be around that arrogant jerk?" Jen ran a hand through her hair, her bid for tranquillity shattered. Pushing up, she grabbed her towel. It was time to get dressed, anyway. All she needed was to get a sunburn, give him more to ridicule her about.

The rest of the day Cole seemed to be everywhere, breaking her train of thought as she sat on the deck, reviewing and revising her interviewing tactics. Though she did everything in her power to put his kiss from her mind, the memory haunted and harassed. Why must the heated recollection of his kiss torture her when he found her so utterly lacking?

* * *

Tuesday's interviews were drawing to a close. Ever since Cole dived into the surf on Sunday, Jen refused to speak to him. Though he burst in the front door several times on Monday and Tuesday, doing his snarling-beast impersonation, she remained angry and resentful.

His gorilla act was completely believable for the interviewees; Jen could tell by their apprehensive pallor once Cole blew in, fitted out with his wicked-looking paraphernalia. Apparently only she could see that under the macho dramatics, her so-called bodyguard didn't give a flying fig about her.

She'd gained a second finalist on Monday. Self-employed wedding and portrait photographer, Jim Wimmer was Jen's age and an avid tennis player. Jen knew nothing about tennis, but she thought she could use a hobby. Maybe tennis could become her passion.

Jim was nice-looking. Blond, laugh creases at the corners of heavy-lidded, brown eyes. His one-sided smile seemed sneering and could be a bit disconcerting, but she was sure she could get used to it. Jim Wimmer was husky and not much taller than she. Because he worked with people, he had excellent people skills, a pleasant personality and positive attitude. Though he'd dressed casually for the interview, he was neat and clean and seemed open to direction. All in all he had possibilities.

Tuesday hadn't gone so well. At four o'clock, Jen could feel a stress headache coming on. She'd had a particularly bad day with particularly bad applicants. First there'd been the sleazy huckster, then the wimpy lap dog followed closely by the human tranquilizer. She was rapidly losing hope that she would find that third finalist she so badly wanted. When her three-thirty appointment left she blew out a depressed sigh. What a condescending pain. If she never heard the phrase "Are we on the same page?" again, it would be too soon.

She heard the crunch of tires and knew her last applicant had arrived. She closed her eyes, throwing out a desperate plea. "Let him be good," she whispered, then arranged her features to look self-assured and optimistic.

When she opened the door a tall, vigorous man smiled at her. For the first time that day, her immediate impulse was not to slam the door in his face. As she introduced herself and walked him to the couch, he told her his name. Van Allison. *Doctor* Van Allison. A man in his late thirties, an anesthesiologist, Dr. Allison told Jen he was tired of putting people to sleep and wanted to try his hand at writing novels. Thrillers.

He joked, "I want to keep people awake for a change."

Jen found herself smiling. *Genuinely smiling.* As the interview progressed, Dr. Allison said he loved to cook, loved children and wouldn't mind being the one to care for them, since he would work on his novel from home. Not only that, he had money enough of his own to afford to retire early, do as he pleased.

He was even enthusiastic about the idea of marriage! She could hardly believe her luck. Handsome, impeccably dressed, urbane and witty, with the same analytical approach to relationships as she had, Dr. Allison became finalist number three in Jen's husband hunt—the decisive front-runner.

When he left at five-thirty, Jen felt hugely restored, vastly reassured about her marriage-between-people-of-like-interests-and-goals philosophy. Tired but exhilarated, she leaned against the door and smiled smugly. "So there, Mr. Noone," she mused aloud. "Even *you* can't call Doctor Allison a fool!"

CHAPTER EIGHT

JEN gulped down a couple of aspirins to try to defeat the headache that had begun to pound behind her eyes. She was finding out the hard way that interviewing a finalist interested in becoming her husband could be extremely stressful.

Kevin waited outside on the deck. He'd arrived right on time, at ten o'clock, wearing Bermuda shorts and a sports shirt. In casual attire, he looked cute and much less reserved than on Saturday. But looking cute in shorts was hardly a deciding factor.

She'd suggested they take a walk on the beach and chat. While she escaped inside to take the headache remedy, he'd begun to remove his shoes and socks.

She had hoped today would be breezy, spontaneous, even fun. But it wasn't turning out that way. She and Kevin were simply not gelling as a couple. She wanted so badly to feel attracted to him. She'd tried, was still trying, though she knew physical allure had not been a critical part of her plan, not even particularly welcome. So what was her problem?

She checked her wristwatch. Two-thirty. Inhaling to prop up her determination, she headed out to the deck. Plastering on a smile, she decided she'd give Kevin one more hour. Walking on the beach, talking about whatever came to mind would be the final exam. She didn't hold out much hope that Kevin would pull out of his also-ran status, but she refused to be pessimistic. Who knew what Kevin might do in the next hour to knock her off her feet—in an intellectual way, of course.

She took Kevin's arm, heading down the steps to the lawn. Out of the corner of her eye she caught movement, instinctively knowing it was Cole. A second later, the sound of a hammer brought Kevin's head up and he, too, located Cole beside his cottage. "What's he doing?" Kevin asked, his expression showing unease for the first time since Saturday.

Jen didn't blame him for his wariness. From where they stood, Cole's broad back and powerful arms, glistening with exertion, were irrefutable evidence of his physical might. Though Kevin was tall, Cole had fifty pounds of muscle on him—not to mention the hammer.

"He's just the handyman." Jen eyed Cole dourly, regretting the thrill she felt at the sight.

"He has kind of an attitude, don't you think?" Kevin asked, keeping his attention trained on Cole as they headed toward the gate.

"Just ignore him."

"It's hard."

She had to agree, but she kept her mouth shut.

"I mean, the other day he gave me a look like he wanted to kill me."

"Oh, he looks that way at everybody." Jen tugged on his arm in an attempt to direct his attention toward the gate, which he was about to run into. "Here we are."

Kevin managed to drag his gaze from Cole, spying the gate in time to keep from colliding with it. As he reached for the latch, Jen's glance flashed covertly to Cole. Just then, he turned from the window frame he was repairing to grab something from his toolbox. He must have noticed them, for he paused and stared in their direction.

Jen had a rash idea. She lay her hand on Kevin's to keep him from unlatching the gate. "I think we should kiss," she said.

"Huh?" He peered at her as though he was sure he'd misunderstood.

"Kiss. We should kiss—to see if we're compatible—*that* way." She lifted her chin, smiling warmly in invitation. "Don't you?"

"Uh—sure." He let go of the gate and grasped her by the shoulders, lowering his lips to hers. Jen peeked to see what Cole was doing. He was still watching. *Good!*

Lifting her arms to encircle Kevin's neck, she closed her eyes. The way Kevin's arms moved around her to draw her to him, his moan against her mouth, the unmistakable signals his lips gave her, all said he was more than willing to take this passionate interplay as far as she would let him. There was no mistaking Kevin McDonnett did *not* find her kiss the inadequate mess Cole had.

Unfortunately, Kevin's kiss wasn't doing a thing for her. The only thrill she felt was vengeful gratification. *So there, Cole!* she threw out telepathically. *You can see for yourself there are men in this world who don't find my kisses boring!*

Deciding she'd better bring the vengeance kiss to an end before things got out of hand and she had to scream for help from the man she was wreaking vengeance on, she slid her arms from about his neck. Pressing lightly but firmly against his chest, she whispered, "That's— enough—thanks."

She held on to her smile, and took his arm. Kevin didn't speak or move. He seemed a little dopey, so she unlatched the gate herself. Clutching his elbow with both hands, she prodded him past the picket fence onto the dunes. Did they look like an affectionate couple?

What difference does it make, nitwit? an annoyed voice in her head demanded. *Why play that bizarre scene for a man you have insisted has no power over you?*

She didn't appreciate the question and opted to ignore it. Gazing into Kevin's eyes, she smiled with all her might. "Don't you just love walking on a beach?" Holding on to her rapt expression, she sternly reminded herself why she was there—to interview for a husband, not to spite Cole.

"I'm allergic to jellyfish stings, so I—"

"How nice," she said brightly, straining to get her mind off Cole. Why was Kevin almost invisible, though she was staring at him, yet her vision of Cole was so sharp and clear in her head? "Tell me, Kevin," she went on, making herself focus on the man at her side, "how do you feel about French arias?"

He stared blankly. Could she blame him? What in the world had made her ask that?

The jerk was finally gone. Cole tossed his hammer into his toolbox and slammed the lid closed. "What a clown," he muttered.

Was this husband-hunting Jennifer Sancroft the same woman whose résumé contained glowing remarks by several of Texas's Fortune Five Hundred she'd brought to the firm as clients? They called her levelheaded, brilliant, always available to clients, confident and reliable in a crisis.

He shook his head, baffled. Rounding his cottage he opened his porch door and set his toolbox inside. "They should see her now," he muttered. "Levelheaded, like hell!" Choosing a husband by placing a want ad was the most asinine thing he'd ever heard. She was making a huge mistake, and by no stretch of the imagination could this plan of hers be called brilliant.

"Just how brilliant have you been lately?" he berated himself under his breath. "Grabbing her and kissing her, then telling her the kiss needed work. That was *brilliant, Barringer!*" Was it because of his belittling that she'd added kissing to her final exam, or was he giving too much credit to his influence over her?

When she and that tall idiot lip-locked beside the gate, he'd found himself staring, unable to move, not believing what he was seeing. And why couldn't he believe it? Did he think just because he'd kissed her that he, alone, deserved the privilege? He winced at his use of the word privilege. "What privilege?" he groused. "Kissing her isn't a privilege, it's part of the job description."

But you weren't applying for the job! a voice in his head jeered.

"Shut up!" he muttered.

The vision of her kissing that skinny guy raged in his head, the memory too tangible. As soon as he'd been able to make himself move, he'd turned away and immediately hammered his thumb. Damn him.

Damn her!

He headed toward the beach and hopped the fence. After trekking over the dunes, he met his duck on the sand. "Hi, babe," he said as the mallard waddled up to him. "Why'd you leave? Did the hammer noise bother you?"

The duck quacked and he found himself grinning. "Maybe I was making more noise than necessary." He squatted beside the bird and stroked its downy head. "That woman drives me nuts."

The duck quacked and shook out its feathers starting from her head and ending at her tail. Cole chuckled. "Yeah, she affects me that way, too."

He stood and went closer to the water. Deciding he needed to exercise his stress away, he shucked off his work boots and socks. Then, damning Miss Sancroft for having such a bizarre affect on him, he doffed his jeans. Naked, he strode into the surf, executing a racing dive into the waves. As he skimmed through the water, he faced the fact that he might have to swim all the way to Brazil to exercise her out of his system. Or was the correct word "exorcise"?

Thirty minutes later he swam back toward shore, noticing someone standing on the beach. There was no mistaking who she was, idling there beside a duck roosted on a pile of denim. In waist-deep water he stood up, shoving hair out if his face.

She squinted at him, her hand shading her eyes. She wore a white, silky blouse and peach-colored skirt. The light fabrics clung to her body in the sea breeze, leaving nothing of her shape a secret. Her figure was curving and regal, nice hips tapering into luscious legs. Her waist was slim, her breasts, firm and high-perched. In the sunset, her loose auburn hair fairly glowed like flame. His gut tightened like an angry fist.

"I thought maybe you'd drowned," she called. "Too bad."

He didn't need sarcasm right now. Vowing to show her how untroubled he was by the sight of her, he put on an unperturbed face. "Is there something you wanted?"

She shrugged. "No, I was just walking."

He cocked his head, eyeing her for a few seconds while she stood there looking unforgivably beautiful. "Well, go on," he shouted. "Don't let the fact that I'm not dead hamper your good time."

She crossed her arms before her. "Are you naked?"

Her blunt question surprised him. "Why? Are you the nudity police?"

She rubbed her hands on her skirt then clasped them. "That's a yes?"

"I guess."

Her mouth dropped open for a second before she regained herself. "Have you no shame?"

He found that question ironic. "Me? I'm not the one interviewing for a husband."

Even from the distance where he stood, and with the sun low in the west, he could see her expression close in a scowl. "For the last time, *my* motives are absolutely pure. Don't change the subject!"

"Okay. You're welcome to swim in the nude, too. It's a free country."

"Yeah, you'd love that!"

"I probably would," he muttered, taking a couple of steps toward her. The water level moved slightly lower on his belly.

"What?" she shouted. "I couldn't hear that."

"I said, I'm coming out." Trying to shake a wayward vision of her romping nude in the surf, he strode another few steps in her direction. The water lapped several inches below his navel. If he knew Miss Priss, the prospect of seeing a naked man tramping toward her would have her on the run in a flash.

Her eyes went wide in what appeared to be shock. "You're not!"

"Why? Do you expect me to sprout fins and live out here?"

She shooed the duck off its denim nest and grabbed his jeans, wadding them. "Here!" She threw them at him, but they fell a car-length short. He headed toward them with no intention of hunkering in the surf to hide his lower half. As he approached the bobbing jeans, he heard her shriek and looked up in time to watch her whirl away.

He felt a surge of satisfaction for being right about her. "Really, Miss Sancroft..." he called as he yanked on the jeans "...for a woman bent on bagging a man, you're pretty skittish about looking at one."

"*You* should cultivate some decency!"

"You should cultivate some common sense." After fastening his trousers, he resumed his trek toward shore.

"Are you decent yet?"

"Absolutely." Rancor sharpened his voice. "Have you cultivated any common sense yet?"

When he reached the water's edge she twisted toward him. "You're biased on the subject because of what happened to your father, so keep out of my business!"

"One man's bias is another man's truth, Miss Sancroft."

"Don't spout platitudes to me!"

"Okay, okay," he said, coming toe to toe with her. "But I have a question."

She cranked her shoulders back and met his gaze like a defiant little general. "Just one? Well, by all means, ask it so you can go away!" She swallowed, and Cole could tell she was not as self-assured as she wanted him to believe.

"How can you respect a man who would marry you for such deplorable reasons?"

She hesitated, looking indignant, even stricken. The glint of distress in her eyes unnerved him. "There's nothing deplorable about choosing a mate with sober logic,'' she said, her face suddenly ashen and sober. ''Facts you can cling to! Emotions just float away! It's safer, cleaner and less messy this way than leaving the decision to things as untrustworthy as hormones!''

Cole was momentarily mute in his surprise. ''Less messy?'' he repeated, curious. ''This logical husband hunt isn't only about granny and grandpa finding love after marriage, or mom and pop, the well-oiled but loveless team, is it?''

The sheen of threatening tears in her eyes betrayed great pain. ''You don't know what you're talking about.''

Damn if he didn't! She had obviously been hurt in the past, terribly hurt, and she never intended to trust her heart again. He experienced a squeezing ache of sympathy in his chest but shook it off. Just because she'd had her heart broken, didn't make this foolishness any more excusable.

''Playing it 'better safe than sorry' isn't always better,'' he said, less gruffly.

''Most of the time it *is* better!''

He shook his head, more pitying than angry. ''Trying to cage your heart is impossible. If you marry one of these finalists for all your logical and emotionless reasons, then what happens on that day you wake up and find yourself in love with someone else?''

''I won't.''

''You can't control falling in love,'' he said. She bit her lip, looking uneasy. A thought struck so he went with it. ''How did today go? Perfect?''

She looked away, apparently no longer able to meet his gaze. ''Not one hundred percent perfect,'' she mumbled. ''But nothing's perfect.''

''Exactly my point.'' Her attention shot to his face. ''Not even the happiest marriage is perfect, so anybody who goes into a marriage based on compromise is a fool.''

She continued to trouble her bottom lip as tears welled. Still, she managed to lift her chin in defiance, an act of courage he found endearing. "Why don't you lecture on the subject of what makes a good marriage," she said, hoarsely. "As a bachelor, I'm sure you're an expert!"

Jim Wimmer's finalist day was ticking to a close. If Jen had been disappointed by her day with Kevin McDonnett, she was wallowing in despair after spending "quality" time with Jim. Though he was personable and intelligent, that sneering, sideways smile bothered her. A ridiculous thing to hang her rejection on. She tried to shake off the shallow reason to mark him off her list, but she couldn't.

He smelled nice, like a crisp, autumn day. He dressed well, was handsome and spoke beautifully. He could cook, though it wasn't a passion. They agreed on governmental and social issues. What was her *real* problem?

"Nothing," she murmured. "I have no problem."

"Did you say something to me?" Jim asked, drawing her attention to him as he sat beside her on the deck.

She felt foolish, mumbling aloud. She shook her head and grabbed his hand. "Let's walk on the beach."

He came willingly. She had the distinct impression that he was still ready to marry her if she chose him. Working on her smile she drew him down the steps to the grass. Once again she saw Cole. He was sawing a piece of wood to repair a second window frame. This time she didn't suggest a kiss within plain view. That had been so childish. She was ashamed of herself.

Her mind slid to last night and Cole's racy rise from the sea. Even in soaked jeans, he wasn't really decent. *The rogue!* His continued pestering, both emotional and physical, was wearing her down. Fortunately for her pride, he did *not* know the extent to which he was harassing her, and she didn't plan to let him find out. Still, his interference was making her husband hunt much more complicated and troubling than she envisioned during the planning stage.

Something he'd said last night rang in her ears. *If you marry one of these finalists for all your logical and emo-*

*tionless reasons, then what happens on that day you wake
up and find yourself in love with someone else?*

Over the years—since Tony—she'd become an expert at
avoiding situations that might cause her emotions to leap
out of control. She'd learned Tony's lesson well. That's
why these weeks around Cole had begun to frighten her.
She couldn't look at Kevin or Jim or even Van with the
open-mindedness she'd expected to be able to. Every time
she tried, Cole's face rushed into her mind, larger than life,
making anyone or anything else too trivial and temporary
to dwell on. *Have you already fallen in love with somebody
else?* she asked herself. *Is that the real problem with your
finalists?*

"It's nice out here on the beach," Jim said, drawing her
from her musings. She blinked, looking around, startled to
notice how far they'd walked from the main house.

She smiled at him with difficulty. "It's gorgeous."

"Just like you." His sneering, sideways smile blos-
somed, sending a tremor of aversion down her spine.

Quit it! Just quit it! she scolded. *It's a distinctive smile!
Many women probably find it sexy!*

"You're a beautiful woman," he said.

"Thank you, Jim." She looked away, dreading what was
coming. *Go ahead and get it over,* she told herself. *A kiss
is perfectly admissible, especially under these circumstances. Besides, it might make all the difference!*

Sucking in a breath she faced him, lifted her chin and
met his eyes in invitation.

He didn't need more encouragement. His lips came down
on hers, hard and heavy and he dragged her to him so
roughly he knocked the breath she'd just inhaled out of her.
In self-defense, she grabbed his arms and pushed, getting
nowhere. She twisted her head. "*Wait,*" she gasped, but
his lips rammed hers, again, making her plea no more than
a distorted noise.

She realized she was being lowered to the sand. Her back
hit hot, grainy earth and a new, terrible knowledge ex-

ploded in her brain. This man thought sex was part of the
final exam. *He planned to take her right there on the beach!*

She pushed at his chest, struggled to get free. When she
managed to turn her head sideways enough to free her
mouth, she cried, *"Stop! Get off me!"* Since he was
sprawled on top of her, crushing her, the command came
out in a ragged whisper.

Ignoring her cry, he grabbed her wrists, pressing her
arms to the sand on either side of her as he rooted for her
lips. "Oh, baby," he crooned. "You don't need to play
hard to get anymore. Just flow with it."

She craned her neck to keep him from reclaiming her
mouth. "Get off!" she cried, this time more ferociously.
"Get off me or I'll—I'll scream!"

He chuckled evilly. "Who's gonna hear?"

She stared, shocked. He actually didn't care that she had
made it clear her answer was no! Suddenly she was angrier
than she'd ever been in her life. How dare he think she
would lie still for this! As he lowered his head to recapture
her mouth, she allowed herself rare free reign over her instincts and bit down hard on his lower lip.

He yelped, and in that instant of surprise, eased his hold
on her wrists. Grabbing a handful of sand, she yanked free
and targeted his face. *"Ouch! Hell!"* He rolled to his side,
his hands flying to his eyes. "You tried to blind me, you
witch!"

Sensing she had only seconds before he cleared his vision, she scrambled out from beneath him and sprinted toward the house. She ran through the deep, soft sand, her
lungs on fire. At last she made the gate. Her breathing ragged and labored, she lurched through it and headed for Cole
as he nailed the new board to the window frame. Reluctant
or not, he said he would be her bodyguard, and for once
she needed one. She'd managed to get away, but if Jim
caught her, and was determined to get his way, she didn't
have the physical strength to fight him off.

"Cole!" She dashed toward him. For the first time she

realized she'd lost a shoe and her blouse flapped open where her struggle had ripped off a button.

He turned around, his expression stern at first, then concerned, then angry. "That *bastard!*"

She skittered behind him. "Is—he coming?" she asked breathlessly as she peered around his broad torso. The answer to her question came into view. Jim barreled through the gate, his face red with rage. He slammed it against the picket fence with a sharp crack that sounded like a gunshot.

"I—I'm sorry to bother you," she said, trying to catch her breath. "But—but…"

"Yeah." Cole shifted his hammer from hand to hand, a move suggesting impatience. "I'll handle it."

He took several steps in Jim's direction as the shorter man lumbered toward them. Clearly furious, he pointed at Jen. His eyes were bloodshot and watery. "I want to talk to her." He lisped a little and Jen noticed why. His lower lip was slightly swollen and starting to bruise.

"Oh?" Cole asked. Jen watched his profile as he held his position between her and Jim, like a great big, sexy wall. "Why?"

"She tried to blind me!"

"Why would she do that?" Cole asked, his hammer clasped in a fist at his side. He didn't look overtly threatening, but something in his stance, his tone, spoke of imminent danger.

"Huh?" Jim asked, as though not expecting the question. "Uh—she's crazy, that's why. She comes on to me then—*blam*—she turns into a frozen fish!"

Jen cringed. She was growing weary of hearing men refer to her that way.

"I see," Cole said. "And which part of 'Get off me' did you *not* understand, jackass?"

Jen was surprised that he knew exactly what she'd said. He couldn't have heard her from that distance. She supposed the situation must be pretty clichéd. There were a lot of jerks in the world like Jim, willing to take advantage of a vulnerable woman.

Fear and anger knotted inside Jen as she watched the two men. She could almost see testosterone fog the air.

Jim glared at Cole; red, weepy eyes shifted to catch sight of the hammer. His features altered from fury to caution as he belatedly registered Cole was not only much bigger than he, but also armed. He opened his mouth to speak, but seemed to think better of it.

Cole didn't take his eyes off Jim. His lips spreading in a smile that looked like the bared teeth of a stalking wolf, he asked, "Miss Sancroft, would you like this moron to leave?" The contrast between his aggressive stance, his snarling expression and the dead calm in his voice chilled her. She wondered if it had the same effect on Jim.

She cleared her throat, whispering hoarsely, "Yes—I would."

Cole nodded. "Tell the lady you're sorry, friend." His feral smile didn't dim and his voice remained eerily calm. "Then you may go."

All the fight faded from Jim's expression and a sheen of panic took its place. Jim broke eye contact with Cole and flicked his gaze toward her. A prickle of fear skittered along her spine. The eye contact was fleeting and ended before his apology drifted across in a mumbled whisper. He twisted away, careening in the direction of his car.

Jen didn't move, hardly breathed, until his car sped out of the drive, spitting gravel. With his cowardly departure, Jen felt a weight lift off her shoulders. Experiencing a wave of gratitude, she turned toward Cole. He stood as he had when Jim stumbled away, watching the dust cloud stirred up by his retreat.

She took in her protector, the inherent strength in his face, his square jaw, visibly tensed. Her gaze drifted to his wide shoulders and powerful, well-muscled body that could move with such easy grace.

She experienced a raw, undeniable urge to show her

gratefulness and walked to him, taking his hand. "Thanks," she said, drawing his solemn gaze. "I owe you."

Why did the unruly thought force itself into her brain that she would be more than happy to pay him with a kiss? She tilted her chin, wondering if he would require more of an invitation than Jim had. She hoped against hope he wouldn't.

He stood there, devilishly handsome, goading her on without a word or action. Or was he simply looking at her? A shaft of sunshine in the dappled shade struck his hair, making it gleam. He was a breathtaking sight, so much so that her heart soared and danced with joy at her good fortune of being near him.

Kiss me! she cried inwardly. *Kiss me like you did last week!*

A strange, burning look flashed in his eyes, as though he'd read her thoughts and might just oblige, but too quickly the image was gone, if it had truly been there at all.

He clamped his jaws. "Don't go through with this stupid business," he gritted out. Brushing past her, he went back to his work.

For a moment all Jen could do was stare after him, forced to witness the play of muscle in his arms and back. After a long, difficult moment, she managed to turn away, feeling ridiculously dejected.

CHAPTER NINE

DR. VAN ALLISON, Jen's third finalist, was absolutely perfect. He had the credentials, the glibness, the intelligence, the "bedside manner" to handle any client she might have to entertain or impress. Not only that, as a wannabe novelist, he planned to work at home. He was amenable to having children and he liked to cook.

He was nice-looking and had money of his own. So why, now that his finalist day was done, did she thank him for his time, shake his hand and send him on his way?

I'll tell you why? jeered a sly devil in her head. *Because he's Mr. Perfect—not Mr. Right.*

Hearing such an illogical allegation whispering through her mind shocked her. She must be insane to send Van Allison away. She hadn't even bothered with the final exam kiss. Not because of the horrible experience with Jim, but because she simply couldn't muster the enthusiasm.

Her thoughts skittered unhappily to Cole. Why was a handyman with a smitten duck, a way of making mint tea, and a smile that could curl her stupid toes, the only man she could see in the "job" of her husband? What happened to her no-nonsense plan for finding a life partner?

She slouched against the front door and buried her face in her hands. She was afraid she knew, but refused to confront it. Hadn't her mindless madness over Tony taught her anything? Didn't she know all too well the folly of choosing a love with her heart instead of her head? Cole didn't have the qualifications to be her husband. No college or advanced degree. He probably didn't own a dress suit and thought a power tie was something you had to plug in to operate.

She struggled to pull herself together. What was she to do? Needing to clear her head, she decided to walk on the beach. She wouldn't be likely to run into Cole. Shortly after Jim's escape yesterday, Cole had left. Jen assumed it was another date. Tonight was Friday. A big date night. She bet Cole would be gone tonight, too. So her walk on the beach would be entirely solitary. Sick to her stomach with the thought of what Cole might be doing at this very moment, she tried vainly to put him and his woman du jour from her mind. "He finds it simple enough to erase me from his!" she mumbled.

She stepped outside onto the back deck and plopped dejectedly in a lounge chair to unbuckle her sandals. She set the shoes aside, padded down the steps and trudged through the gate. She felt weighed down, exhausted, ineffective and weak-willed. "Jen, you idiot," she grumbled. "You had the perfect candidate right in your hands, and you let him go."

She took a deep breath of sea air, fighting the urge to cry, to pound her fists on the sand. She cursed herself for losing focus so completely, and cursed Cole for being a troublesome and oppressive fly in her ointment. If he hadn't been there, if she'd never met him, she would be with Van Allison, *this minute,* planning her marriage.

Trapped between Van, the man she needed, and Cole, the man she wanted, she felt desolate, torn, rootless. Too soul-weary to remain standing, she sank to the sand, hugged her knees and stared out to sea. The surf's boom, usually calming, jarred her. Somewhere in the great, black sky a seagull shrieked, and she nearly jumped out of her skin. She dropped her chin to her knees and closed her eyes, breathing deeply, trying to repair her shattered confidence. The effort failed miserably.

She'd run out of candidates and time. Next Thursday was her meeting with the all-powerful J. C. Barringer. In order to present him with her husband she needed to have a candidate by now. The first half of next week had been reserved for applying for a marriage license and dealing with bureaucratic red tape. If somebody didn't magically materialize between now and Monday morning—well, the ugly truth was, she needed a bona fide miracle if she was to be married by Thursday's dinner meeting.

She heard sloshing that hadn't been part of the night noise a moment before. Lifting her head she looked toward the sound. She was startled to see someone rising out of the sea, and experienced the surreal light-headedness associated with déjà vu. It was Cole. Only this time, she was relieved to observe he wore his black swimsuit.

She was amazed he wasn't out somewhere on a hot date, and experienced a wayward rush of relief. She hated herself for it, but she couldn't squelch her joy. She was thankful— no, she was crazily delirious—that he wasn't someplace else making love to some other woman.

He was almost upon her before he noticed her. She could tell because he came to an abrupt halt less than two feet away. "Whoa!" He wiped wet hair out of his eyes. "I almost stepped on you."

Wrapped in her cocoon of depression, she gazed up at him, wishing the dim moonlight didn't pay such unrelenting homage to his body.

"What are you doing out here?" His broad shoulders heaved as he breathed, exhibiting the exertion he'd expended during his swim.

She shrugged, lowering her gaze to the sand. "I just felt like…" She didn't quite know how to finish that sentence. He didn't care about her troubles, and she had her pride. "I just felt like sitting." How lame. But she *was* sitting. That should satisfy his idle curiosity.

"Sitting in the dark, huddled in a ball?" he said. "Something's wrong, isn't it?"

She didn't appreciate his ability to hit the nail on the head. "Everything's peachy," she muttered. "I'm sitting in the dark, huddled in a ball, because I like sitting in the dark, huddling in a ball. If you have a problem with that, then *tough!*''

He didn't immediately respond, but neither did he leave. "I see."

She was startled when he took a seat beside her. "So what brought on this giddy adventure? I assume you're engaged to be married and this is your version of bubbly merriment?"

She was in no mood for his needling, so she lied. "Yes. This is how we frozen-fish types celebrate getting engaged."

"Hmm." He draped an arm about one knee, eyeing her with skepticism. "So which one is the lucky winner, Tall-and-Skinny, Sex Maniac or Smiley?"

Resting her cheek on her knees, she looked at him. "I'll have you know, Smiley, as you call him, is a medical doctor, witty, charming and—and absolutely perfect." She couldn't maintain eye contact and turned away to stare out to sea.

"So the winner is Smiley."

New anguish seared her heart. Why did he have to rub it in? "That's none of your business."

The crashing surf was the only sound for a long, strained moment before he spoke. "Why are you so down? It sounds like you've had great success. Why aren't you thumbing your nose at me and saying 'I told you so'?"

She flicked a look at him, battling to conceal her misery from his searching stare. His expression was somber, and she thought she detected a dangerous hint of sympathy in his eyes.

As emotionally fragile as she was, the sense that he might feel the urge to comfort her was too disturbing to deal with on any sensible level. She was suddenly overwhelmed by the emotional chaos she'd suffered these past two weeks. No longer able to lie, or hide her sorrow behind a brave face, she shook her head. "I didn't choose any of them." Her voice quivered.

Humiliated, she wiped the backs of her hands across her eyes to brush away fugitive tears. "I'm not giving up," she hastily added, refusing to let him see the depth of her despair. Clutching at control, she cleared the quiver from her throat, but couldn't quite look him in the eye. "I believe in myself. I believe I *can* make this happen."

"I don't understand," he said. "If the doctor was so perfect, what made you turn him down?"

She shook her head, unable to form words and keep her voice from breaking.

"It's harder to use another human being for personal gain than you thought?"

"I was not going to *use* anybody!" She cast him a dour look. "And since you refuse to understand that, I don't intend to explain anything to you." She would endure the tortures of the damned before she would tell him how much her wayward attraction to him had played in her failure to pick a husband.

"If you think you can still find a husband, what do you intend to do, beg on the streets?"

Though her courage and self-confidence were in shreds, his cynicism made her angry. "If I have to, I will!"

He watched her in silence and she found the experience both terrifying and seductive. The planes of his face looked very angular in the false light. He could have been carved from stone, but for his eyes. A look of intense, clear light, glimmered in their depths like cut crystal.

He watched her with unblinking concentration. She was intrigued and unsettled to find herself so utterly the object of his attention. The sensation of completely occupying this man's notice wrapped her in a strange but welcome glow, the likes of which she'd never known.

That discovery frightened her, yet her self-preservation mechanism refused to kick in. She could only stare back, basking in his steadfast observation. Once again, she thought she detected a flash of compassion. Even if it was only a trick of the dim light, and completely erroneous, she couldn't help feeling somewhat restored. It was amazing how his silent companionship could renew her, even when she was mad at him.

An idea ruffled through her mind like wind on water, so delicately at first she couldn't quite admit it into her consciousness. As the seconds and minutes ticked by, with Cole's gaze fixed so completely on her, his unwavering attention sent a surprising flood of bravery coursing through her.

"Will *you* marry me, Cole?" She was stunned at how calm her question sounded to her own ears. It was as though she'd thought the question through and found it absolutely sane. She hadn't thought it through, and knew it was anything but sane, yet somehow that reality hadn't been enough to keep her quiet.

Her impromptu marriage proposal hung in the air between them, a volatile stillness engulfing the night. Jen couldn't even hear the crash of surf, she was so focused on Cole's face. Though she knew what his answer must be, knew how he felt about her and about her husband hunt, she was filled with anticipatory adrenaline, like a little girl full of childish hope, about to find out if she could go to the circus.

He blinked, clearly stunned by the question, then frowned at her. "I believe in love, Miss Sancroft, even if you don't."

I'm afraid I love you, she threw out telepathically. She didn't want that to be true, and she would certainly never voice it. So she merely stared back, fighting the stirring effect of his eyes.

Time oozed by so slowly that its movement could hardly be detected. She swallowed hard, but true to her philosophy of "there is no success without risk" she made herself ask, "Are you saying you will?"

The sea rose up and growled around them, agitating Jen as she waited, preparing herself for his refusal. So many long, dawdling seconds plodded by she could not suppress a despairing sigh.

"Are you saying you love me?" His voice was flawlessly reasonable, as though he were showing her how passionless her marriage proposal had been, and how thoroughly he disapproved.

The condemnation hit hard. The last thing she wanted to admit—*to even think*—was that she loved Cole Noone, and she persisted in fighting the possibility. He was nothing like the husband she was looking for. He was not driven, not a corporate climber. He was a plain-spoken, smug handyman, climbing nowhere and not caring.

The answer to his question should be a resounding, even laughable, *no!* Sadly, the thrill she felt whenever he walked into a room, or rose unexpectedly from the sea, was too strong, too debilitating, to be anything else but love.

Her pride refused to let her reveal such a devastating truth to a man who found her utterly lacking, both as a professional and as a woman. Doing her best to be convincing while protecting her pride and her heart, she leaned toward him, laying her hand lightly on his arm. "Look, Cole, I—I trust you. I respect you."

His gaze slid to her hand resting on his arm, then lifted to her face. "You respect me?" He smiled in a cool, unmirthful way that didn't pretend to cross the chasm separating them. "Forgive me if I don't believe you. Don't forget, I know your attitude about advanced degrees and super achievers. You may be desperate, but you're laying it on a little thick, even for a backward handyman to swallow."

"No, no." She squeezed his arm, trying to shore up the gorge she'd dug with her unthinking snobbery. He was a takes-no-bull man who believed she was a neurotic bubblehead incapable of dispensing anything *but* bull. If she'd ever had an impossible job, this was it. Still, she forged on. "Many corporate wives don't have degrees, are simply 'housewives,' and are perfectly capable of conversing with business bigwigs.''

His eyebrows rose in obvious astonishment. ''You want me to be your corporate *wife?*''

The breeze shifted and his scent washed over her, sensually male with a hint of the ocean brine that sparkled on his torso. The combination of sight and scent made it hard to think, and she needed to remain clearheaded if she planned to persuade Cole to take on the job of being her husband. Well aware of his contempt, but too far into it to turn back, she hurried on, ''I didn't mean wife, literally! You're great at household things. You cook.'' She had a thought and voiced it. ''You do want children, don't you?''

He clamped his jaw, as though incredulous that she would ask such a question, or that she could possibly be serious. After a long pause, he said, ''I'd like to have children—eventually.''

She experienced a wild thrill, refusing to recognize his obvious scorn. He was still there, still talking, wasn't he? ''Don't you see, we could make a good marriage,'' she said. ''With respect and trust—and you'd have security, since my job pays very well.''

He frowned at her. The long pause could have been considered insulting, if she had allowed any room in her plan for hurt feelings. But she hadn't. She couldn't permit him to reject her.

''I have no intention of being used to boost your career,'' he said at last.

She felt a stone fall through her heart. Who was she kidding? Cole would never marry her. Too drained to argue further, she nodded to acknowledge his rejection. She had blocked the stark eventuality of it from her mind as long as she could, but no more. Conscious of a dull throb of grief in her temples, she lay her cheek on her knees and watched him. ''You don't even respect me, do you?'' she whispered.

* * *

Jennifer Sancroft looked at Cole with something very fragile in her eyes. His stomach tightened. He had a feeling he would remember the affliction in that look, this moment, for a long time to come.

He couldn't seem to take his eyes off her and he grew furious with her for making him care. He fought his soft feelings, his urge to make love to her. He was determined not to be held prisoner in a one-sided love like his father.

He was dismayed to see her bite her bottom lip, tears welling. *Hell.* What was he doing here? Why was he listening? "I don't respect what you've been doing, Miss Sancroft," he said, less gruffly. "I imagine, in your work, you're good at what you do."

That wasn't an empty assumption. Last night he'd met with the second vice president and his wife. Comparing Jennifer Sancroft's résumé with the other two candidates, she would make a good president.

"I'm not just good at what I do," she retorted abruptly. "I'm exceptional at what I do." She faced him, clearly incensed. "As a matter of fact, I'm the only person qualified for the top job."

He didn't respond, just watched, impressed by her passion.

"You don't understand why I want to find a husband before my interview," she said. "Well, whether you like it or not, I'll tell you why. Because it's insulting to know I'm better at something than those around me, yet I expect to be passed over, as I was two years ago when the last president was chosen." She ran a hand through her hair, a jerky, violent move. "It kills me that I could be passed over again for something as irrelevant as my marital status!"

Though he'd read her résumé, and knew her credentials were exemplary, she didn't know he knew. As a handyman, he wouldn't be aware of her job qualifications, probably wouldn't care. But as J. C. Barringer, he was interested. He wanted to hear her explanation. "What makes you think you're so much better qualified?"

Her expression stony with conviction, she said, "The company built its reputation on tax litigation. I'm better at that than anybody else. I have a passion for it. It's my area of expertise, my background. With me as president we can get justice for our clients. Under the last president, the company lost focus, diluted emphasis on tax problems. Neither of the other candidates has my understanding, my competence, my devotion or my record of success with the Internal Revenue Service." She met his narrowed gaze straight-on, unflinching. "And lastly, getting the presidency would announce to the world that I've *finally* achieved what I deserve. That's only human, isn't it? To be recognized for your accomplishments?"

Her kiss had hinted at great passion within her. Now he could see it in her face, her bright, wide eyes, and hear it in her voice. "You make a good case," he admitted. "Why not march in and tell the old coot what you told me, instead of perpetrating this husband hunt?"

"I told you why!" she said. "I've been passed over before, with no more justification than the fact that I was the single female. I can't change my sex, but I can—"

"That's bull," he broke in. "If you're as perfect as you say for the job, any CEO in his right mind would choose you. There's more to it."

"Of course there's more to it," she retorted. "I've been telling you that from the beginning, but you've refused to believe me!"

"What?" he asked. "That nonsense about making a real marriage and family, discovering love through like interests and beliefs?"

"Yes!" She eyed him with fiery triumph. "You finally get it!"

"I not only don't get it. I don't believe it."

"Well, don't. I don't care. But just for your edification, my career has kept me very busy. I—I love what I do, but that doesn't keep me from wanting a home and family of my own. So I decided if I could find a husband who would help me get the job, then, with our like beliefs and goals, I could have a family, too. And—and eventually even fall in love.''

He opened his mouth to respond, but she plunged on, giving him no opening to argue. "I'm in my thirties. I've given my whole life to my career. This might be my last chance to start a family. As a woman president with babies of my own, a major concern would be helping employees who are young mothers with their needs. The firm could vastly reduce expensive turnover in support staff with innovations like job sharing, paid maternity leave and on-site child care. In order to become president, initiate these programs, and to take advantage of them myself, I need to look settled—be settled.''

"So you figured you'd advertise for a husband.''

She glowered at him, resentful. "Would it have been more virtuous or honorable if I cruised singles bars, indulged in chancy, one-night stands, lost sleep, let my work and possibly even my health suffer?''

He found the question reasonable, and that surprised him, but he played devil's advocate. "So you decided to exchange one extreme for another?''

"My time was limited and called for extreme measures. I had to move heaven and earth to get these three weeks for the entire search, courtship and wedding.''

"Maybe you're not being fair to this man or any future children, if you're that wrapped up in your work. How can you expect to have a personal life?''

She frowned at him. "I told you, by making the company family friendly.''

"In other words, you'll have time for your family, just not to find a husband in the normal way?''

"What's normal? And who cares, as long as it works?''

"It didn't work.''

He could tell his remark hammered her. She seemed to

shrink and sag. Breaking eye contact she rested her chin on her knees and stared into the darkness. After a long pause, she whispered, "It could have."

He heard the hushed statement and wondered what she meant. "Excuse me?"

She shook her head. "Nothing. Never mind."

He watched her, saw the change from defiant to defeated, and felt unaccountably responsible. "So, you're back to square one," he said, almost gently.

She pressed both hands over her eyes as if they burned with weariness. After a moment, she turned to look at him. "You could get a divorce," she said, so quietly he wasn't sure he'd heard correctly.

"What?"

She took a shaky breath. "I said you could get a divorce. I know how you feel about being in love, so I—I'm not asking forever of you. Just do me this favor, for a little while. I don't even ask that you quit dating other women. You don't have to tell anybody we're married. It can be just—on paper. You can end it anytime, after next Thursday." Her voice grew steadier with conviction. Her eyes had gone so wide with supplication and hope they seemed to swallow him. "Go with me as my husband to my interview with J. C. Barringer. Help me show him I'm settled, with a husband who can hold down the home front. Make him see I'm solid, traditional presidential material— good enough even for a closed-minded old coot!"

Close-minded old coot! What would she do if she knew she was asking to be Mrs. Close-minded Old Coot?

"I thought you said this could be your last chance to have a family. Asking me to be your temporary husband cuts the heart out of your plan, doesn't it?"

Her face clouded with distress. "This isn't what I planned, but everyone thinks I'm on my honeymoon. I'm committed." She looked up at the sky. "At least, I'd have the job I deserve. I'll be in a better position to establish family friendly working conditions and achieve justice for our clients.'' She met his gaze again, looking rueful. ''There's something to be said for having meaningful work.''

In other words, to get the job, she was willing to use him and lie about their relationship at her upcoming interview. For a moment he'd thought, even hoped...

He shook off the foolish notion.

Wishing she weren't the type of woman who would stoop to such tactics, though she refused to admit it even to herself, he made a decision, possibly a very stupid one. He wasn't quite clear on his reasoning. Those tragic eyes were messing with his mind, not good for cool, prudent thinking. He hoped like hell he was contriving her day of reckoning, not making the same mistake his father made, a mistake Cole had sworn he would never make.

''All right, Miss Sancroft,'' he said, feeling like he was standing on the sidelines, watching a stranger who looked like him acting out this bizarre drama. ''I'll marry you— on paper—for a while,'' he ground out, ''and I'll go with you to meet the old coot.''

She stared, her eyes huge and luminous, a disturbing sight for a man determined *not* to take her in his arms. His gaze lingered on her face, those bewitching eyes, then slowly moved over her body, pausing on the creamy expanse of her neck. He had a wild urge to nuzzle her there, kiss the soft, pale flesh. A voice in his head reminded, *You've agreed to marry her, but you can't kiss that sexy neck. You don't want to! You're making a point, not a commitment!*

He stood up, knowing he'd better put distance between them. ''I'll be gone this weekend,'' he muttered, needing space to clear his head. Maybe he would jet off someplace, have some fun, get his attitude adjusted. Besides, if he planned to marry Jennifer Sancroft as ''Cole Noone,'' he needed fake ID. With his diverse contacts, that wouldn't be a problem, but it would take a little time. ''Meet me at the

Corpus Christi courthouse, eleven o'clock, Monday morning.''

She stared up at him with those big, glistening eyes, and opened her mouth to speak.

''Damn it, woman!'' he cut in. ''If you thank me, the deal's off!''

CHAPTER TEN

"THERE'S something to be said for having meaningful work," Jen mumbled to herself. How many times had she told herself that since Friday night? "There's something to be said for having meaningful work."

There was, wasn't there! She must keep her head on straight. Cole had promised to marry her, *for a while,* not forever. She stood very still, trying for composure. She'd fought so hard to keep from falling in love with Cole. But she had fallen in love. A sensation of foreboding shot through her with the shocking insight that this truly would be her one, *and only,* marriage, however brief. Because after Cole there could be no other man for her.

She tried not to dwell on how desperately she wished things were different. With all her heart she wished he didn't think of her as a self-centered user. How sad that accepting his offer to be her temporary husband, she had only reinforced his belief that what she was doing was purely selfish. Little did he know the only reason she'd failed in her original plan to find a life mate was because she'd fallen so hopelessly for him.

Yes, she was in love, and she had no business being in love. Even if Cole hadn't found her detestable, he was wrong for her. But try to tell her heart that! She'd certainly tried. She'd tried all weekend. She'd tried on Monday, Tuesday and Wednesday. She'd told herself that very thing more times than she could count. She'd never thought of herself as a stubborn person, but this being-in-love-with-Cole thing had her defeated. She could see no way out. Even her memories of Tony paled by comparison.

Today was her wedding day. Even knowing the folly of

it, she couldn't squash her fluttery, breathless anticipation. Telling herself she was the biggest fool ever born, she took special pains to look as pretty as she could—like a real bride—in the trim, white suit she'd purchased in Corpus Christi the day before. She smoothed her hand over the silk fabric. White silk. It was perfect for a wedding dress, but utterly unsuitable for work. Considering she would probably never wear it again, buying it had been a crazy extravagance. But she'd wanted everything to be so—so real. She was a very traditional woman, and wearing white was a beautiful ritual, an age-old symbol she couldn't give up. Not even knowing the wedding was little more than a farce—at least to Cole.

Her mind rambled back to Monday when he had met her in the courthouse. He'd filled out the paperwork then left, muttering something about an emergency porch repair job in Houston. The last thing he'd said was that he would meet her at the courthouse at eleven o'clock, Thursday morning, for "the ceremony."

He hadn't even said the word "wedding." She sighed, trying to ward off the depression that threatened to overpower her. Cole couldn't have made it clearer how despicable the idea of marrying her was to him. His brusque, unsmiling appearance at the courthouse had caused a heaviness to center in her chest where it lingered all week. The few minutes he'd spoken to the courthouse clerk was the only time he'd smiled, pretending to be a happy bridegroom. Otherwise, his demeanor had been grim and silent.

Jen scanned herself in the mirrored wall over the bathtub, noting the sorrowful shimmer in the shadow of her eyes. She blinked to clear away the sheen of tears. No matter how evident he'd made his feelings for their temporary marriage, Jen couldn't control a wayward, romantic need to make it as authentic as possible.

The slim suit she'd chosen was the picture of chic romance, with its cowl neck blouse of delicate lace. For tradition's sake, she slipped on a pair of antique, garnet earrings that had belonged to her beloved grandmother, as her "something old." From her jacket's breast pocket, peeked a blue silk scarf, her "something blue."

She had nothing she could call her "something borrowed." She looked around, concerned. She must think of something. What could she borrow, and who could she borrow it from? She'd called Ruthie, wanting a friendly face at the wedding, even though Texas law didn't require witnesses. Unfortunately, her ex-assistant hadn't been available to come. Both her children had chicken pox, her husband was out of town on business and her in-laws had hightailed it back to Wichita Falls the instant the first chicken pock showed itself.

She recalled Ruthie's guffaw when Jen confessed who her new husband would be. No matter how exhaustively she'd tried to explain that her choice had been a desperate, last-ditch and *temporary* thing, Ruthie just kept on laughing. Apparently Ruthie sensed Jen had succumbed to the old bugaboo "love" and was delighted to the point of hysteria. What she didn't seem to comprehend was that Cole had done no such succumbing.

Unsettled by the reminder, she pressed a loose strand of hair that had fallen into her eyes back into her smooth chignon. "Well, you *look* like a bride." She stared bleakly at her reflection. "Not a happy bride, but—" To her dismay, her voice quivered and broke.

Angry with herself for becoming so low—on her wedding day—she straightened her shoulders. Okay, this was *not* the storybook wedding she envisioned in her little girl daydreams, and *not* the no-nonsense union she'd planned from her husband hunt, but it *was* her wedding day. She had not failed—at least in her plan to marry or her time schedule.

Whatever happened after the ceremony, well, that was up to the fates. She'd done everything she'd contrived to do—*except*, a voice inside her head whispered, *you are marrying a man you shouldn't marry, and you're marrying him for love—a reason you mistrust and deplore!*

The irony pressed down on her. She'd intended to make a real marriage, learn to care for the man she chose through their mutual regard. Instead, she was marrying a man she had fallen madly, irrationally in love with, a man she would soon have to let go. That fact should ease her mind, but instead it tore at her heart. Tonight, after the interview with J. C. Barringer, Cole Noone would walk out of their marriage—and her life.

The doorbell chimed, startling Jen so badly she gasped out loud. Who in the world could be at her door? The only "guests" she'd had since arriving nearly three weeks ago had been her interviewees. With one last swipe at that wayward wisp of hair that seemed insistent on falling into her eyes, she headed out of her bedroom and dashed down the stairs.

She checked her watch. Nearly ten-thirty. If she planned to get to the courthouse by eleven she needed to leave. On her way to the front door, she grabbed her white shoulder bag. She would quickly deal with the doorbell ringer on her way to her car.

She threw open the door. "Forgive me, I'm in a hur—" During the second it took her to get halfway through her sentence, her brain registered the fact that the man standing in the shade of her covered porch was Cole.

At first, she cast off the absurd idea. The man before her wore a sage-green, silk jacket, white T-shirt, pressed vintage jeans and boots. It never occurred to her that Cole owned a jacket, let alone one made of silk.

But there was no mistaking those eyes, bright, pale, framed by jet-black lashes. It was Cole, all right. Her heart tumbled over itself at the sight, her gaze drifting back over his clothes. She could hardly believe what she saw. The combination of rugged and ritzy was sexy, romantically eclectic, and on Cole, somehow more elegant than any tuxedo. Though she found his attire appealing and macho, she was a bit dismayed that he chose such nontraditional garb for his wedding. Her rejoicing heart sank at the idea that his choice of clothes only reinforced the fact that, to him, their marriage was a contemptible deception. Why should he take it seriously?

Her annoying inner voice nagged at her again. *Exactly! Why should he take it seriously? This wedding is nothing but a momentary glitch—at least as far as he's concerned.*

"You're ready," he said, his tone somber. "I'd expected to have to wait."

His assumption that she would put him out even more than she already had shook her out of her lamentable stupor, and she recovered her ability to speak. "I was just on my way." Her voice trembled and she berated herself for her vulnerability to his nearness. "I thought you said you'd meet me at the courthouse."

Those iridescent eyes lingered on her face, seeming to take in every detail. She felt like a painting in some museum. What an odd thought.

"If we're going to make dinner on time," he said, "we'll need to head for Dallas from the courthouse. It's a good six-hour drive, even pushing it. No point leaving one of our cars in a public lot."

She saw the logic in that and felt stupid she hadn't thought of it herself. Sadly, she hadn't been thinking logically recently. "I see." Gathering control, she indicated her car. "My suitcase is in the back seat. Mind if we take my rental?"

He shook his head. "Why add mileage? I'll move your bag to my car and I'll drive. Somebody from the rental agency can pick up your car here."

She would have argued, but decided against it for two reasons. First, he made a sensible point about the mileage. Second, her fabric-covered high heels weren't the best for driving. Without further comment, she retrieved the house key from her shoulder bag and locked the front door. When

Cole took her arm to aid her descent down the steps, she was startled and jerked away. "I can walk!"

She wasn't sure why she resisted his touch so vehemently. He'd only attempted to help keep her from falling on her face. Obviously, her wounded pride had brought on that outburst. Because Cole found marrying her such an abominable chore, she desperately needed to find his touch equally abominable. Or, failing that, make him *think* it was.

The drive to Corpus Christi embodied the stoniest silence Jen ever endured. She hugged the door on her side of Cole's four-wheel-drive vehicle, trying to absorb herself in the scenery of the central coast drive, its distinctly tropical feel, with breeze ruffled palm trees, sand dunes and sea oats, then farther off, shell-laden beaches.

Today it was all so much dust and cardboard. Her whole focus remained riveted on the brooding man beside her, his sharp profile, bronzed by wind and sun, his square jaw, muscles working.

During the tense thirty minutes she had plenty of time to try to find things besides Cole to concentrate on. She took scant notice of his plushly outfitted car. Clearly this disdainful handyman bachelor chose to squander his hard-earned cash on big-boy toys, like his recreational vehicle with its leather interior and what looked like a fancy stereo system. Too bad he chose not to fire it up it for this trip. She'd grown fond of French arias. Even if she hadn't, she could use a little noise.

They sped across Harbor Bridge, the two hundred and fifty foot cantilevered structure that signaled the end of their journey was upon them. Jen knotted her hands in her lap, trying to hold on to her fragile control. She shifted her attention to Corpus Christi Beach, nervously scanned the bustling marina teeming with sailboat masts. A cargo ship caught her eye as it slowly moved into port.

They reached the end of the bridge and she looked ahead to take in the city skyline. Her heart hammered and she felt dizzy. Was she really about to get married or was this all a crazy dream?

Moments later the ten-story, limestone courthouse came into view, with its unique amber, octagon windows. Cole drove past a shimmering, two-story waterfall and a green-belt with oak trees and shaded benches. Pulling into the parking lot he stopped the car and got out without comment. She watched him stride around the front of the vehicle toward her side. As he approached, she glimpsed the twinkle of a watch chain dangle between a belt loop and his front pocket. When he reached her door, she had her nerve up to ask him one more, tiny favor.

He opened her door, the grim but polite bridegroom.

"Uh…" She pointed at the chain. "I wonder if you'd let me borrow that to use as a bracelet?"

He bent to peer into the car, appearing as though he hadn't understood. "You want to wear my pocket watch as a bracelet?"

"Just the chain. For the wedding." She felt silly having to admit to Cole her desire for tradition, since he felt so— so *nothing* about their wedding. But it was important to her to make the ceremony as genuine as possible. Her heart so badly wanted it to be. Bravely, she forged on. "I have something old, new and blue. I need something borrowed. I didn't think a silver tray from the beach house would look very good balanced on my head."

He watched her with narrowed eyes. It infuriated her that he would find her request so difficult to grant. "It'll only be for a few minutes. I won't try to steal it."

"All right." He sounded resigned. Straightening, he extended a hand to assist her from the car. She didn't want to accept, but climbing into the extra-high vehicle had been a struggle in her slim skirt, so she gave in. Her common sense told her it would be preferable to arrive at the ceremony without a broken ankle. "Thanks," she murmured as she took his hand and he helped her manage the long step to the pavement.

When he let her go he turned to unfasten his chain from his watch. "It'll fit around your wrist twice."

"That's okay." She extended an arm. "I appreciate this."

"No problem." He stuck the gold watch back in his pocket and unfastened the clasp from his belt loop. As he did, Jen noticed a charm or medallion dangling from the end of the chain. He held it out, wrapped it twice around her right wrist and clasped the two fasteners together. She held it up and shook her wrist. "Thanks. That'll be just fine."

"Whatever," he said, jaw muscles flexing.

"What's this?" She fingered the bauble on the chain, turning it toward her. Before he could answer she recognized it as a long-venerated symbol of a scholastic honor society. Jen herself had belonged to the same society at the University of Texas. "Where did you get a Phi Beta Kappa key?"

He flicked her a quick, sharp look, then glanced at the charm she fingered. "What?" he asked, his glance returning to her face. "Oh—is that what that is? I won the watch in a poker game. That doodad was on the chain."

She was confused. "And the guy you won it from let you have it?"

Cole's brows dipped. "Maybe he figured he'd win it back."

"But he didn't?"

His lips twitched cynically. "What does it look like?"

He had a point. She shrugged. "Well, I know I wouldn't trade mine for anything."

"Yes, you would," he said.

"Why do you say that?" she demanded.

His lips lifted in a smile, however mocking. "Look what you're doing for a job. If you think you wouldn't have traded that chunk of metal for a promotion and saved yourself all of this, you're a liar."

She dropped her arm, unable to argue the point. The

chain jingled, the Phi Beta Kappa key dangling in her palm. If she'd known all the emotional turmoil being around Cole would cause, she might have parted with her key to avoid it. Even so, she couldn't let him have the last word. "I would *hate* to think of my Phi Beta Kappa key in the clutches of some arrogant know-it-all who could never grasp all that it signifies!"

"Don't get hot under the collar, Miss Sancroft," he ground out. "I'm not after your precious little key." He took her elbow, urging her forward. "Come on, let's get this done."

At precisely eleven o'clock Jen and Cole stood in a windowless courtroom, all alone. Jen couldn't think of a thing to say and Cole didn't seem inclined to chat, either. He leaned against the judge's bench, arms folded and stared out over the mustard-yellow chairs that comprised the visitor's area. His expression solemn, he seemed to be looking inward, preoccupied.

Jen made herself look away to absently scan the wood-paneled judge's bench. It was presidential-looking with the United States flag, Texas flag and Texas state seal displayed on the beige wall above it. Her skittish glance slid to the jury box, outfitted with six leather chairs. Only six? "I wonder what kind of cases they try here?" she murmured.

"What?"

Her gaze flicked to Cole. "Uh—nothing. I was thinking out loud."

He looked at her intently for a moment, then turned away, his jaw tightening.

Against her will, she continued to stare at him. Why did he have to look so fabulous—tall, tan, dark eyebrows slanted in a frown over spectacular eyes. In that classy sage, silk jacket, vintage denim and hand-tooled, leather boots, he was the image of some moody, anti-chic model, impatient for a photo shoot to end.

Jen heard a noise and shifted to watch a lanky, mustachioed judge enter from a rear door, his black robe fluttering. Smiling, he got the pleasantries over swiftly, then took a position before his bench. He indicated that they come together to stand before him. Jen moved forward from the visitor's area, and Cole relinquished his sexy slouch against the bench. When they drew together, their eyes clashed, his awe-inspiring, even filled with conflict.

She hurriedly transferred her attention to the judge. He opened his leather-bound book, his expression growing serious as he began to read the solemn rite. With deliberation and distinctness, he uttered the words that would bind Cole and Jen in lawful wedlock.

Jen listened to the familiar passages, spoken with sedate dignity. Inside her head she screamed *Yes, yes, yes* she would love, honor and cherish Cole for the rest of her days. *Yes, yes, yes,* she would adore him always and forever, in sickness and in health. To every ceremonial instruction and cherished vow she cried, *Yes, yes, yes!* inside her head. But to her ears, to the judge's and Cole's, her promises were the shy whispers of a blushing bride.

Cole answered softly, too, his promise to hold her in his heart for all eternity was spoken gently, earnestly, almost passionately. She cast a glance at his face. His brow was creased with what looked like the deep concentration of a bridegroom centered on his vows. Knowing what she knew, Jen feared the expression was more likely loathing for their lies.

His eyes, however, were what drew her. They burned with a fire of such dramatic proportions she caught her breath. She wished the flames that leaped in their depths were an expression of an emotion more heated with ardor than anger, but she was too sensible to believe in miracles.

She felt a ring being slipped on her finger, and looked down to note that Cole held her hand in one of his while he slid the ring on with the other. The act, though only a touch, was so dear to her, it was a bond unto itself. She silently pledged again her foolish, everlasting love.

A diamond solitaire sparkled and twinkled on her ring

finger, making her blink. She hadn't thought to mention to Cole that he'd need to get a ring, and she was surprised he'd remembered. Square-cut and at least three carats, the jewelry looked quite realistic, for a fake, which it had to be. Even imitation diamonds of that size and quality were awfully pricey for a handyman to afford.

She smiled at him, the effort tentative, but real. Though she appreciated the fact that he'd remembered a ring, she relished the warm strength of his hand holding hers much more. When he let her go, she experienced a sense of loss, but kept smiling at him, trying to convey her thanks for the effort he'd taken, even if the ring was booty from another poker game.

When it came time for her to give him his ring, she reached inside her breast pocket and retrieved the golden band she'd purchased when she'd bought her dress. Eighteen-carat gold, it was as real a wedding band as any bridegroom ever received. A foolish indulgence, she knew, but tradition was tradition, and she so wanted Cole to…well, dwelling on it was a stupid, painful exercise in futility.

As custom dictated, she took his hand. His fingers were much steadier than hers and she prayed she wouldn't fumble and drop the band. She slipped it on his finger without mishap and breathed a sigh of relief.

She was gratified her guess at size was correct. It fit perfectly. Cole's wedding ring was neither a fake nor gambling loot, but the genuine article—bought for the man she loved. Unable to look into his eyes, she made herself release his hand and return her attention to the judge.

The black-robed magistrate nodded, smiled and went on with the ceremony, oblivious to the fact that he was an unwitting accomplice in a con.

Jen fingered the wedding ring on her finger, battling tears. She berated herself inwardly. *Cole is doing what you asked of him. He doesn't love you. Face it once and for all! Get the dratted promotion and try to move on with your life!*

"You may kiss the bride."

The judge's decree didn't penetrate into Jen's troubled consciousness. Only when Cole stepped close, took her by the shoulders and turned her to face him, did she grasp the significance of those five words.

You may kiss the bride.

He was actually going to kiss her! How often had she prayed for this moment? She met his gaze, hoping the raw longing she felt didn't show in her face. His stare was bold. The flame in his eyes set off a flutter in the pit of her stomach. Was he angry at the necessity to kiss her, or was it arousal she saw?

Her lips ached for his touch, had ached for another taste of his kiss for what seemed like an eternity. She didn't care which emotion she saw in his eyes. She was insane not to, but she didn't. Her heart pounding with need, she lifted her chin.

In the next instant his mouth covered hers, his kiss surprisingly gentle. Relishing the warmth, the texture of his lips, Jen began to sense a hunger below the surface, belying his outward forbearance. She experienced the heady sensation that he was holding himself in check for the benefit of their audience. But the heated message came through, sweeping over her in the shattering subtlety of his kiss.

His hands did not move from her shoulders. He held her almost chastely as his lips pressed against hers, moved gently, leaving their lusty message to burn into the sensitive flesh of her mouth. What was he saying with his slyly erotic kiss?

Did he feel more for her than he cared to admit, or was he playing with her? Was he loathe to kiss her deeply, to admit his attraction, or was he only toying with her, driving her mad for his own entertainment? Was he so angry with her for this plot that feelings of attraction or no, he refused to admit he cared? Or was this his diabolical way of punishing her for the scheme she had involved him in?

Refusing to taint the moment with doubts, she slid her

arms about his waist, beneath his jacket, hugging him to her. She told herself any bride would hold fast to her husband during the blessed wedding kiss. No matter what Cole's underlying feelings might be, he couldn't argue that. The pretense must be completed, whether he liked it or not.

If she never held him in her arms again, she would have this moment to keep in her heart. He felt so solid, so vital, and he smelled like sunshine in a pine forest. She inhaled him deep into her, clasped him to her breast, delighted in the thud of his heartbeat against the tremble of her own.

Exalting in his delicious maleness, Jen was suddenly aglow. She tingled where their bodies touched. His heat was intoxicating. Blood roared in her ears, thundered through her heart and made her weak in the knees. She never dreamed any mere coming together of lips could cause such a hot tide of passion, but she was wild for him— so in love she couldn't bear the thought of letting him go. She clutched, moaning against his mouth.

The raw, feral sound shocked her. It must have shocked Cole, too, for the next instant he ended the kiss. Though he didn't relinquish contact with her shoulders, he drew a step away.

She felt insubstantial, her body burning from the wild sweetness of his kiss. Her breathing came hard as she met his gaze. What she saw stunned her. Unuttered pain was alive and smoldering in his eyes. *Pain.* So clear and dramatic it cut her to her core.

CHAPTER ELEVEN

THEY drove in silence toward Dallas. The pain in Cole's eyes monopolized Jen's thoughts, a tragic memento of a kiss that, for her, had become the most significant event of her life.

He sped along the highway, his concentration totally focused on his driving. At least he looked totally focused on driving. She wished she had the capacity to be totally focused on *anything* but Cole.

By three o'clock, she could no longer stand the strained quiet. She cleared her throat. "You haven't asked about your duck."

He blinked, as though being brought back from some distant place. "What?" He peered her way for a second, then returned his attention to the road.

"Your duck."

He frowned. "Oh—right. How is she?"

Jen stared blankly out the window, watching the flat prairie land and its lazily grazing cattle whiz past. "She has a suitor. Right after you left a boy duck started following her around like a lovesick idiot." She winced at the phrase "lovesick idiot," but shook it off.

"Drake."

She eyed him uncertainly, wishing her heart didn't do a pirouette of gladness every time she saw his solemn, handsome profile. "Excuse me?"

"A boy duck is a drake."

She experienced a stab of disappointment. This wasn't a conversation, it was a tutorial on waterfowl nomenclature. "Actually—I don't care." She unclasped her hands and shifted to more fully face him. "I thought you should know how easily females can get *un*-smitten over you."

He cast her a perturbed look. "What is that supposed to mean?"

She had no earthly idea. Refusing to admit it, she shifted to stare out the windshield. "Just—you—think about it!" *Ha!* Let him assume she was so deep she'd just inflicted a complex, obscure truth on him that had whooshed over his head. She was the smug one for once, and allowed herself a small smile.

"Do you want to stop for food?" he asked.

She hadn't eaten all day, and her dinner meeting with J. C. Barringer was hours away but she couldn't stand the thought of food. She was too tied up in knots. She shook her head and glanced his way. "If you're hungry, feel free."

He pursed his lips but didn't respond. It appeared the ride would be a long, silent test of wills.

She looked down and noticed his watch chain around her wrist. "Oh..." She unfastened it and held it up. "Here's your chain back. Thanks."

He released the steering wheel with one hand and took it from her. "No problem."

"You might think about giving that Phi Beta Kappa key back to its rightful owner."

He shifted his hips slightly and slid the chain into his jeans' pocket.

She hated it when he didn't answer. It was so rude. But could she blame him? He was far from happy about what he'd done for her; he didn't like her personally. And here they were—married. Even amid all the dishonesty and intrigue, her foolish heart thrilled. For the moment, at least, she was pledged to Cole Noone as his bride.

Working to regain her composure, she faced him, determined to tell him she was grateful, even if he bit off her head. "Uh—Cole," she began. "I know you told me not to thank you, but—"

"Jennifer!"

"Don't interrupt!" She held up a halting hand and forged on, though her heart took note that he'd called her by her first name. "I owe you my thanks, and you're going to get it, whether you want it or not." She fought the charisma he exuded, even as hostile as he was. He uncurled his fists from around the steering wheel as though to ease a cramp, then clutched the wheel again.

"Look, Cole," she went on. "All I want to say is, if there's anything I can ever do to repay you, don't hesitate to call. I mean, if you find yourself needing repair jobs, I'll be happy to refer you to friends. I can vouch for the fact that you do good work. As a matter of fact, I'll go one better than that. I'll do your taxes, for free. For *two* years!"

"Don't make any rash promises."

"Don't be so stubborn. Why shouldn't I?"

"Your important dinner meeting with J. C. Barringer is tonight. How do you know I won't humiliate you?"

Was he actually worried he wouldn't live up to her idea of a good corporate husband? How absurd! She couldn't believe she'd ever had any doubts about him. "I'm not worried, Cole." She smiled at him, an expression never more heartfelt than at that moment. *You fool,* she nagged inwardly, wishing she could wipe that sappy smile off her face. *You fought so hard, determined not to fall irrationally in love, again. But you did! You even committed yourself to him, whether he believes it or not. If there were only some way you could convince him not to get that divorce you promised him. If he'd only give the marriage a little time!*

Wanting badly to create some trust and mutual respect between them, she went on, "You're smart, witty, and in many ways as cultured as anyone I know." *Besides,* she added inwardly, *you're the man I love. You could stick the edge of the tablecloth down your shirtfront and use it for a bib, and I wouldn't care.* Aloud, she added, "I have complete faith in you."

"Your confidence is heartwarming..." He peered her way; something unnerving flared in his eyes. "...darling."

Cole parked in front of the Trinity River restaurant, so angry with himself he could spit nails. He'd been furious for days. How could he have allowed himself to fall in love with a woman who would get married to advance her career? Even his mother hadn't been that devious.

How could this have happened? He'd counseled with himself for years *not* to fall into the same trap that swallowed up his father. Yet, here he was, married to a woman who thought of him as some sub-par specimen of male she'd resorted to using at the last moment. Most unbelievable of all, he'd gone along with it. Why? What had possessed him?

An inner voice scoffed, *You know exactly why and exactly what possessed you!* Cole strangled the steering wheel as the annoying voice jeered, *You stupidly fell in love with her, you idiot!*

It made him furious. He was furious when he'd left her on the beach last Friday night. He was furious when they'd applied for the marriage license, and he was furious today when he'd found himself on his way to pick her up for the ceremony. That hadn't been the plan, but he'd needed to see her. And when he had—*Lord* she was beautiful, the very image of the virgin bride. He'd had a hard time keeping his hands off her. Well, he hadn't quite managed it. He'd tried to take her arm, but she'd resisted, reminding him of how unsatisfactory she felt her final choice in husbands had been.

Waiting for the judge, he'd seethed, continuing to fight an internal battle with himself about *why* he insisted on being such a blithering idiot. The only time he'd felt some degree of sanity was during the ceremony. It was ironic and nuts and beyond comprehension, but he'd spoken the vows from his heart, meant every word. *Blast him,* he had!

What happened in the next few minutes inside that restaurant would be the second stupidest thing he'd ever done—after the wedding. He wondered what twisted chunk of gray matter had convinced him that agreeing to marry her would take her down a peg. She might be a little angry for the deception, but ultimately what was he really doing that would be anything but a relief to her?

Clenching his teeth, he ran a hand roughly through his hair. No point in second-guessing now. The path was set. He had to know—

"Cole?" Jen's questioning tone broke through his stormy musings. He aimed his contemptuous gaze her way. She winced at his expression but pointed vaguely in the direction of his chest. "Uh—I'm not sure they'll let you in without a tie."

He glowered at her for another heartbeat before opening his car door and flipping the keys to the smartly uniformed valet. "Why don't we see," he ground out. Trinity River restaurant was another of Cole's Dallas properties—a fact his too fastidious bride was unaware of. The truth was, whatever J. C. Barringer happened to be wearing on any given evening *became* the dress code.

The valet murmured respectfully and stepped out of Cole's way as he rounded the car to get Jen's door.

The doorman smiled and nodded courteously. Cole was startled when Jen allowed him to take her arm as they ascended the marble steps to the leaded-glass doors. Once inside Jen took the lead, marching to the podium where the tuxedoed maître d' watched over the reservation book. "We're with the J. C. Barringer party," she said authoritatively, under the mistaken impression she was in charge.

The maître d' lifted his gaze over her head to Cole, giving a respectful nod of recognition. Cole dipped his brows and shook his head slightly, a cautionary signal for the man to say nothing to him. Without missing a beat, the maître d' returned his gaze to Jen and smiled agreeably. "Yes, certainly." He indicated that one of the wait staff approach and whispered instructions, then turned to Cole and Jen with a smile. "Please, follow the waiter." Jen preceded Cole. She was several steps ahead when the tuxedoed maître d' murmured, "So nice to see you, sir."

Cole nodded, though his mind churned with plaguing thoughts of what was to come.

Jen looked back, apparently having heard the maître d'. "What did he say?"

Cole shrugged casually and lied. "He said, 'Have a nice meal.'"

Jen seemed to accept that and hurried after the waiter. Cole watched her as she walked. He knew her well enough by now to know she was nervous; her gait and her back were both a little stiff. He experienced a twinge at what he was about to do. *Hell,* he told himself, *you have nothing to feel guilty about. She begged you for the marriage, and you won't hold her to it. She has nothing to lose.*

Another voice whispered perversely, *but how she deals with the truth could do you serious harm, Barringer.*

"Shut up," he muttered.

"Did you say something, Cole?" Jen faced him, the look in her eyes seemed genuinely concerned. He shook off the impression and took her arm, deciding it was a trick of the twinkling chandelier above their heads. "Not a thing."

The waiter showed them to a secluded table in a romantic corner. Romantic! Where did that thought come from? This was the exact corner where he'd met with the previous two vice presidents and their spouses. The waiter stood by respectfully as Cole helped Jen with her chair then took his seat beside her. One white taper, set in a sterling candlestick, flickered in the center of their snowy linen cloth.

"Would you care for drinks?" the waiter asked.

Jen looked up, "Just coffee please. Black."

"Two coffees." Cole motioned him away.

The waiter nodded and left. Cole turned his attention to Jen as she look around absently. From her anxious expression he didn't think she was registering much of the luxurious interior, with its low-light chandeliers, lustrous marble floor and walls, sterling accents and vivid artwork.

Soft classical music and the murmur of the richly dressed clientele served as pleasant background noise. Cole could see Jen wasn't interested in the opulent trapping, the melodious concerto or her fellow diners. She was straining to see one person, and only one person, when he arrived—the old coot. Of course, not knowing what he looked like made it difficult for her. He could see frustration in her expression and the rigidity of her body language.

"I thought he'd be here," she said, confirming Cole's guess. She shifted to face him, looking nervous but beautiful in the candle's glow. She smiled and he felt a jab of desire. "Don't look so gloomy, Cole." She reached over and squeezed his hand, resting on the tabletop. "You are absolutely…"

She faltered, appearing embarrassed, as though she'd spoken out of turn. "What I mean is, I have a good feeling about tonight." She continued to squeeze his hand and smile at him. "I made the right choice," she said, her gaze almost shy. He didn't know how to take her remark. He'd expected her to tell him not to eat with his fingers or something. Her compliment was out of the blue. After another second when he didn't respond, she released his hand and looked away, her smile fading. "I wish he'd get here."

Cole noticed their waiter returning with a pot of coffee. About the time he finished pouring, Jen would realize there were only two places set at their table. He fisted his hand that rested on the table, feeling time closing in on him.

Jen checked her watch. "It's two minutes till seven. We're a tiny bit early." She looked up at him and smiled again. It was almost as though his being there gave her courage. "I refuse to worry. Everything will be fine."

Why did it grind his gut to have her look at him that way? *Because she trusts you, jerk! She thinks you're here to help, but you're about to pull the rug out from under her.*

The waiter moved soundlessly away then returned, pouring water into their crystal goblets. When he was finished, he came to a polite halt beside Cole, offered them two gold-embossed menus. "Would you and the lady care to hear the chef's signature entrées for this evening, Mr. Barringer?"

There it was. The truth, quietly and simply laid bare. He only had to wait for Jen to grasp it. And react.

His eyes never leaving Jen's face, he shook his head and waved the waiter away.

Her smile dimmed, her expression becoming puzzled, then uneasy. She flicked her glance from the retreating server to Cole, then to the table and its two place settings and finally back to his face.

For a long moment she sat woodenly, saying nothing, though he sensed she was beginning to grasp the enormity of the situation. Slowly her eyes took on the unblinking, glassy stare of a frightened deer.

"You?" she whispered at long last.

He could almost hear it rip—the fabric of her trust—torn forever. He willed himself to become a stone, defying the need to take her in his arms. "The old coot," he said with a slight nod, as though introducing himself. "At your service."

She lifted a trembly hand to point. "*You're* J. C. Barringer?" Her voice had risen an octave and he could barely hear her above the music and buzz of voices.

First would come the anger, then the relief of knowing she hadn't shackled herself and some stranger in a loveless marriage. He nodded. "Incredible coincidence, don't you think?"

"But—how? Why?" she whispered. Even with her recent suntan, she looked excessively pale.

He'd expected anger by now. It seemed her fuse was longer than he'd anticipated. "The beach house was mine before it became a corporate getaway, and June was always my month," he said. "It was leased to you by mistake."

"Why didn't you tell me?"

That was hard to answer. He feared it had more to do with her wide, green eyes and the sexy pout of her lips than he cared to admit. Instead of the truth, he told her the same lie he'd told himself. "It was a test—to see if you had what it takes to be president."

"You let me make a fool of myself!" she cried under her breath.

Here it came—the righteous anger.

"You let me go on looking for a husband to impress— *you!*" Her lips trembled.

She looked more stricken than angry, surprising him. "I told you my feelings about that," he said.

"I can't believe you…" The fact that he'd gone through with the marriage ceremony evidently leaped into her consciousness, because her eyes grew huge and swam with tears.

Tears?

"Then why did you—" She clenched her fists. *"Oh— my—Lord. Why…"* A tear lost purchase on her lower lashes and slid down her face.

Cole winced. He'd known she would feel betrayed, but he'd expected her to explode with rage. He hadn't expected her to be so—so sad. He had never seen a sight so hard to take as that lone tear. Now he understood how helpless his father had been, how there was no safe haven from love. His passion for her was a living, breathing thing, and he had neither the strength nor the will to kill it. His misery was so acute he had to fight to keep from howling like a bloodied wolf.

She would laugh if she knew all the facts, understood who the indisputable fool was in all this. "Why did I go through with that wedding?" he finished for her, cursing himself for not having a cool, calculating answer. The truth was that he was a human being with human frailties. It wasn't her fault that he'd fallen in love with her any more than it was his. Regardless, he would carry the scars for a long, long time. "I married you—to show you how foolish and unnecessary it was." It was a feeble and an outright lie, but it was all he had. "I'm giving you the presidency, Miss Sancroft."

Her lips parted in surprise. "You—you...?" She faltered, stared. The silence became drawn-out and heavy. Finally, after a couple of false starts, she murmured dully, "You're giving me the presidency?"

He exhaled wearily and nodded. "You had the best qualifications all the time—without going to the ridiculous lengths of advertising for a husband."

"But—but if you're..." She paused, the image of a woman coming face-to-face with a harsh reality. "People will think I got the job because I married the boss."

He had trouble looking into those woebegone eyes, exhibiting the tortured glimmer of broken faith, but he forced himself to remain outwardly stern. "Don't worry about that. You have the power to keep that from happening."

Her expression was like someone who had been slapped hard in the face. Clearly she didn't understand. He didn't expect her to. A choking sound issued up from her throat and she covered her mouth to smother it, her expression wretched. She looked like she might be ill.

He experienced a gambit of conflicting emotions. He was afraid his desire to take her in his arms was winning out and he steeled himself against it. "You have the job, without the need to commit your future to a loveless marriage. I'd think you'd be relieved."

"You'd think...?" The sentence died on a strangled sob. She sat so rigidly for so long he feared she'd stopped breathing. At last, she whispered brokenly, "Of course, that's what you'd think."

He sat back, surprised he felt like such a worm. He'd lied to her, true, but he'd given her the job she wanted with hardly a downside. Why wasn't she dancing on the table? Why did she sit there with a glazed look of despair on her face?

Masking his inner turmoil with cool indifference, he pressed the flats of his hands on the tabletop and stood. He needed to get the hell out of there before he pulled her close, kissed those trembling lips and begged her to be another whole kind of woman. This wasn't fantasyland.

"Congratulations on the promotion." Dragging his wallet from an inner jacket pocket, he fished out a fistful of bills and tossed them on the table along with the valet stub. "You use the car—darling. I'll take a cab. Enjoy your celebration dinner. You worked hard for it."

She hugged herself as though she'd grown suddenly cold. Trembling, she stared off into space and rocked back and forth in her chair. She seemed to be looking inward at some disastrous scene. Tears welled and spilled down her cheeks.

His heart lurched, but he fought any softening. She deserved to suffer, considering she'd planned to foist a temporary husband off on "the old coot." But he couldn't stand seeing her hurting, looking so small and forsaken, transformed from the positive, determined, spirited Jennifer Sancroft he knew. He hated himself for his part in this tragic change in her. *Blast it,* he growled inwardly, *you have nothing to apologize for! She begged you to help!* So why did he feel the need to ease her mind? He'd planned on having his lawyer explain things, but he couldn't leave her like this. "Pull yourself together," he chided, angry with himself for his vulnerability to her. "You have nothing to lose in this and a great deal to gain—even more than you can guess."

She flashed him a dazed look. Her cheeks glistened with tears and the sight tore at him.

"About the fake name," he went on, "Texas is still the Wild West where marriage is concerned." Her eyes had a troubling, glazed look. He wasn't sure she was comprehending anything, but he felt compelled to go on. "Try to hear this, Jennifer. It's true I married you as Cole Noone, but according to Texas law, that doesn't change the fact that we're legally Mr. and Mrs. J. C. Barringer. And since Texas is a community property state, half of everything I earn from today forward is yours.''

His voice was strange to his ears, his words flat and mechanical as he explained, fighting to remain outwardly cool. ''Since I was the dishonest party, using an assumed name, and because you married me in good faith—at least as good as your motives allowed—you have the legal upper hand to choose to remain married to me, or—not.''

He kneaded his temples; his brain was heating up. It was hard to pretend indifference, watching her lovely, stricken face. ''The ball's in your court,'' he said, sounding slightly hoarse. The strain of his pretense was beginning to show. ''I've given you all the power. Have the thing annulled or remain my wife. It comes down to your degree of avarice.'' His last glimpse of her huddled posture and tragic, lost expression tore at his soul.

He strode away, a man stripped of victory, with nothing left inside but self-doubt and pain.

CHAPTER TWELVE

FROM the moment Cole walked out of the restaurant, Jen had been drowning in despair. His betrayal left her wrecked, body and soul. The irony gnawed at her. He had married her when she'd asked him to and he'd given her the job she wanted, yet she felt betrayed and abandoned.

As far as the other employees thinking she'd been given the presidency because she'd married "the boss," Cole had certainly left her a perfect way out so that would never happen. He'd said the ball was in her court. She could stay married or get the thing annulled. He'd made it all very straightforward and simple. A quick, quiet annulment, and nobody would ever know. Then why—when she'd gotten everything she'd gone after—did she feel trapped at the dead end of hopelessness?

Because you loved him, and he did nothing but lie to you. Be grateful for the job. Get the annulment, do the things for the company you want to do and forget him!

Monday morning, bleary from lack of sleep and feeling like the walking dead, she forced herself to go in to work. She feared Cole would show up personally to announce her presidency. She was sorry to discover she was right. He arrived practically on her heels, heartbreakingly handsome in a classic navy suit and vivid power tie. No longer Cole Noone, the shirtless handyman she'd fallen in love with, he was J. C. Barringer, the archetypal captain of industry.

He stood before the assembled employees, looking like the rich, tough-minded, successful businessman he was. He set them at ease with a joke, an easy laugh and a dazzling display of white teeth. His startling, light eyes magnified the inky blackness of his lashes and the deep bronze of his tan. Hating herself, Jen stared longingly at him as he made the announcement of her presidency and beckoned her forward to be congratulated.

She moved to the front of the assemblage in a daze. Cole's handshake was formal, his hand warm, but his eyes held the flash of contempt only she could see.

His hand holding hers sent waves of unwelcome desire washing over her. Her heart skipped again and again, making her dizzy. Tugging her fingers from his light grip, she fought to hold on to her composure. By some miracle, she managed to get through her acceptance speech, though she had no memory of what she said.

After her brief remarks, Cole added a shocker. During the transitional period he would take a more "hands-on" interest in the firm. To Jen's dismay, he chose the office next to her own, making it impossible to keep from running into him a hundred times a day. If he'd decided to punish her for her husband ruse, his brutally seductive presence was devilish torture.

She suffered agonizing bouts of déjà vu—once again in love with a boss who had betrayed her. Once again, she was forced to be near him while fighting to ignore and forget him. Only this time, Cole made no sly attempts to seduce her as Tony had. On the contrary, Cole's private glances were cool, his touch, accidental and quickly withdrawn.

Always a private person, Jen managed to sidestep queries about her marriage and honeymoon. No one knew she was Mrs. J. C. Barringer. Cole was certainly not letting on. So she merely informed associates she was keeping her maiden name for business reasons.

The victory she'd wanted so badly, maneuvered so desperately to secure, was hollow. All too often she was forced to run head-on into the man she'd foolishly fallen in love with, only to witness glittering reproach in his eyes. She'd thought him a handyman and she'd fallen in love with him. To discover he was everything she'd hoped for in a husband—and he *was* her husband, *but he loathed her*—was too cruel a trick for the fates to play.

A week plodded by, each day worse for Jen than the one before. Cole was too often nearby, chairing meetings she had to attend, dropping by her office to confer on this or that, his troubling eyes, his stirring scent, making her lose her train of thought. Since his invasion, she couldn't recall completing a full sentence in his presence. She certainly didn't feel like she had, blathering fool that she'd become.

When he was away from the building she could function logically, and began to initiate the changes she'd had in mind to improve working conditions for employees with children, and revamp client support. Sadly, whenever Cole came on the scene, she returned to babbling like a brook. She almost wouldn't blame him if he were rethinking his decision to make her president.

Friday evening, after a long, trying day under Cole's contemptuous scrutiny, she collapsed on her sofa, the granddaddy of all headaches coming on. Too sick at heart to eat, she lay there, one arm thrown over her eyes.

She hadn't begun the annulment process, couldn't bring herself to do it. Which was nothing if not self-destructive, since each day the danger grew that someone would find out Cole was her husband. And worse, each day she delayed she knew what Cole thought—that she was a grasping female after more than just the presidency of a small Dallas accounting firm. He thought she was after money and position, too. Which wasn't true at all.

"I love you, Cole," she whimpered to the emptiness. "How can I make you see that?"

She fingered her wedding ring, then clenched her hand in a fist. Why did she wear it? Why hadn't she simply taken it off as soon as Cole divulged his true identity? Then at work she could have told those who asked about her wedding and honeymoon that she and her secret fiancé called it off at the last minute. She knew exactly why she hadn't done that. She *wanted* to be Cole's bride—his wife—

through all life's ups and downs. The ring was a symbol of something she desperately wanted to be true. Idiot that she was, she couldn't seem to part with it. Not yet.

What she didn't understand was why Cole continued to wear his wedding band. Was it to remind her of the foolishness of her ploy, or of the depth of his deception?

The phone rang, jarring her. She cringed, the piercing noise intensifying the throb in her head. Without sitting up she fished around on the end table for her cell phone. On the fourth ring she located it and picked it up. "Hello?"

"Hello, Jennifer, this is your mother."

Jen rubbed her eyes. "Hi. What's up?"

"I'm going back to school and I thought you should know."

Jen grimaced, confused. "School? I don't get it?"

"Your father is retiring as Birchfield's president in September and my involvement with academic functions won't be needed, so I've decided to study psychology, become a clinical psychologist."

"A what?" Flabbergasted, Jen sat up and stared at the phone. "What on earth for? Haven't you had a full career at the college?"

Her mother made a guttural sound that was as close to laughter as her restrained personality would allow. "What career? I was helping your father with his career. Now I intend to have one of my own."

Jen was confused. "But—I thought you loved the college faculty teas and alumni luncheons, the committee work and—"

"I did that for your father. I love him and I wanted to be all the help I could be. But that was not me. I want to be a psychologist."

Jen was speechless for a long moment. She'd never heard her mother actually say the word "love" about her dad before. "Really?"

"Don't you think I would make a good psychologist?"

"Oh—oh sure, I meant—you *love* daddy?"

There was a long pause. "What kind of a question is that? Of course I love your father."

Jen closed her eyes to shut out the light, hoping it would help ease her throbbing head. "Well—I mean, of course you do, now. But you didn't when you got married, right?"

Another pause. "What on earth are you babbling about, Jennifer?"

She rubbed her eyes. "Well, I mean, you and daddy have so much in common, and you're never—I mean, I've never even seen you hold hands. I just thought you were one of those couples who married for compatibility rather than passion."

"What an odd thing to say," her mother remarked. "Where do you think you came from, the 'newborn' shelf in the grocery store?"

"Of course not. I just…" She shook her head.

There was another long pause. "Jennifer, I realize your career is your first love, but if you're thinking of marrying someone because you both belong to the same political party or enjoy Debussy's music, well, as your mother, I feel it's my duty to caution you off such an idea. Marriage is hard enough without—"

"No, Mom," she cut in, having heard that same lecture from Cole too often to endure it again. "I'm not—considering—that." She hadn't wanted to inform her parents about her husband hunt until she'd found a suitable finalist and set the wedding date. Now she was doubly glad she hadn't mentioned it. Looking back, she knew she'd been so stubbornly determined, she wouldn't have listened to their objections. Even after proving her wrong about the basis for their relationship, she'd have no doubt clung to the idea that her grandparents had married out of need rather than love. She'd have bulldozed on with her husband hunt, possibly even causing an estrangement between her and her parents.

When her "compatible mate" plan hadn't worked out and she made the temporary marriage deal with Cole, she certainly hadn't wanted her parents involved. She could just see that wedding invitation, "Dearest Mother and Father, please come see me marry a man who doesn't like me, a man who is begrudgingly doing me a favor, so consequently we won't be married longer than absolutely necessary." Yeah, sure.

"Is everything all right, Jennifer?" her mother asked.

Jen inhaled for strength. Hardly anything was all right. "Oh—did I tell you I've been promoted to president of D.A.A.?"

"My gracious, that's fine news. But of course you deserve it." Her mother paused. "Why don't you sound delighted, Jennifer?"

Jen grimaced. Her mother would make a good psychologist with such sharp perceptivity. "Um—well, it's a little complicated." She wanted to pour out her heart to her mother, but she felt like such a fool. "It's just that…" She heaved a despondent sigh, too worn down to be wise. "Mom, what would you do if you were in love with somebody, and you married him—knowing it wasn't a real marriage, just on paper and for a short time…" she sucked in a shuddery breath and hurried on "…and knowing he didn't love you. He was just doing you a huge favor. And—and if you told him you wanted to stay married, even told him you loved him, he would have reason not to believe it, and think all you really loved was his money? What—what would you do?"

The phone was quiet for a long time, making Jen so agitated she had to ask, "Mom? Are you still there?"

"Yes, Jennifer." She paused again. "I was just trying to understand."

"Yes—well, I'm not sure I do."

"I think…" she began slowly "…I'm going to have to take a few psychology classes before I can begin to answer that."

Jen made a pained face. "A few abnormal psychology classes, you mean."

"This isn't you, is it?" her mother asked, sounding troubled.

Drat, she knew she shouldn't have said anything. It was her problem, not her mother's. Always so disciplined and deliberate, she would never have gotten herself into such a crazy situation. "No—it's—nothing. A friend did something very stupid, and now she's stuck in a tricky catch-22," she lied.

"I see. Well, she certainly is." The pause was decidedly uncomfortable. "Jennifer, let me know when this friend decides what to do. I'd be interested. I wish I could be of more help."

"No problem." She bit her lip. Her mother wasn't buying the lie one hundred percent, but neither could she quite believe her logical, level-headed daughter would have done anything so idiotic. "I'll let you know what—my friend decides."

Jen hung up the phone and laid back. The conversation had done nothing to ease her aching head. As she lay there, her distress over almost telling her mother everything subsiding, she began to ponder the surprising revelation that her mother had sacrificed her own desire for a career all those years to assist her father—*for love.* They might not have been a lovey-dovey-kissy couple, but they were a well-oiled team *because* they loved each other, not because of mutual goals and interests.

Maybe her grandparents had been the exception that proved the rule. Or maybe they'd fallen in love before they married, and simply didn't grasp the truth until later. Who knew? She'd been in love with Cole long before she'd admitted it to herself.

She pressed the heels of her hands to her eyes. Too late, she understood the all-important element—love—had been missing from the power couple she'd tried to create. At long last, she could see what a colossal mistake it had been, attempting to arrange another human being's life to suit her wants and needs. How selfish and shortsighted she'd been.

She obviously hadn't valued herself enough to trust the CEO to recognize that she deserved the position.

And how right Cole had been!

His deception had actually done her a favor. How wrong it would have been to bind herself to a person she didn't love, on the off chance love would grow. She was ashamed for her foolish naiveté. She owed Cole her thanks for saving her from herself. Though he'd married her, he certainly hadn't bound her to him. His caustic parting words at the restaurant rang in her memory, "Have the thing annulled or remain my wife."

The *thing.*

A week and a half of unrest and discontent had come and gone since Cole's marriage to Jen. He'd taken the afternoon away from the accounting firm and returned to his corporate headquarters to do some business, get a break. Mainly he needed some head-clearing distance from his bride.

Ruthie Tuttle, Jen's ex-employee, was at a seminar in Houston this week. She didn't yet know her new boss was Cole Noone, the handyman. She only knew her new employer had been on a monthlong vacation.

Having the corporate personnel manager hire Ruthie out from under Jen the way he had was a mean trick. But he'd been angry with Jen and he'd been looking for a new executive assistant of Ruthie's caliber—as well as a way into the house where Jen held her husband interviews. The choice seemed perfect in more ways than one. He looked forward to seeing Ruthie's face when she found out he was J. C. Barringer. She had a great big, healthy laugh that was utterly refreshing. He knew the moment would be entertaining, when it came.

Unfortunately that was the only thing he looked forward to these days. He certainly wasn't thrilled about these next few minutes. His attorney, Mike Byrne, had dropped by his office after a six-week European vacation, so Cole broke the news of the marriage and its unorthodox circumstances.

Cole watched the lawyer prowl back and forth across the carpet, hands clasped behind his back. Any second now he expected Mike to erupt like a volcano. It wouldn't be pretty.

"What possessed you, Barringer?" he bellowed, his paunchy face crimson. "Were you crazy drunk or crazy in love?"

Cole rested a hip on the corner of his hand-carved oak desk, staring at his apoplectic attorney without responding. The answer was too painful.

"Lord!" Mike exhaled wearily. "I can't believe it! No prenup! And you married her under a false name, yet!" His voice was sharp and brittle, cracking like weathered wood. "She has you by the short hairs, man! Do you have any idea how much money you make in blue chip dividends alone every *week*?"

"Of course," Cole muttered.

"I've never known you to do stupid things. Why didn't you call me, get my advice? You had my London number!"

"I wanted information, not a lecture," he said, frowning. "So I asked a professor friend who teaches family law at Texas Law College. I knew what I was doing."

"I simply can't conceive of that," Mike shouted, purple with rage. "If you were going to do something so stupid, why did you even bother with a ceremony?" he spat sarcastically. "Why didn't you just live with the woman and *call* yourself man and wife. That would have been enough, since Texas law is so damn relaxed about matrimony, it also recognizes common law marriages. At least you wouldn't have the fake name complication!"

"She wanted a ceremony." Cole shrugged. "But speaking of common law marriages, you know my property east of Corpus Christi? For three weeks before the wedding, we—"

"Don't even say it!" Mike threw up his hands as though blocking a blow. "I'm not hearing this!" He glared at Cole, his eyes bulging. "Are you aware that during these last ten days you've been married, your *wife* can already take a small fortune to the bank?"

Cole blew out a breath, exasperated. "That's not the point, Mike. Cut the drama queen act."

"Not the point! Not the point!" the lawyer shouted. "Then what is the point, man? Under Texas law, using a fake name made you the deceiving party, so she has the legal right to choose to remain Mrs. J. C. Barringer or not. You've given her *all* the options!"

"I know that."

"Just out of morbid curiosity, what on earth made you use a false name?"

"I didn't want her to know who I really was."

Mike's exhale was a dark curse. "That makes perfect sense. Why would you want your *wife* to know who you are?" he jeered. "And on that subject, where did you get fake ID?"

Cole lifted a brow meaningfully. He had no intention of divulging that information. "Let's just say I have friends in low places, and leave it at that."

Mike clenched his fists and made a strangled sound of frustration. "You're insane, man! What possessed you to *purposely* dig yourself such a deep hole? How could you risk so much?"

Cole stared Mike down. For a moment all he could hear was the thunder of absolute silence. Then, from somewhere far away, a siren stretched across the distance to them. He looked toward the sound. Outside his office window another day was dying. Street lamps, straining to hold back the gloom of night, cast orange, shadowless light on the Dallas cityscape.

The siren faded. Once again the heavy silence began to thunder in Cole's head. He shifted to scowl at his attorney. "How could I risk so much?" he repeated, as lucid and resolved as he had ever been in his life. "You don't know the half of it, Mike," he said. "I'd risk everything."

"You'd risk everything?" Mike bellowed, incredulous.

Cole knew marrying Jen hadn't been the smartest decision he could make. It had been the *only* decision. Sadly, even vowing it would never happen to him, Cole had every reason to believe he was caught in the same hopeless trap of unrequited love his father had been caught in. The only way to find out was to give Jennifer Sancroft everything she could possibly want and the power to keep it. As his lawyer had pointed out, the ball was now in her court. "Yes—everything," he muttered.

Mike blustered, shaking his fists ferociously. "You *are* crazy!"

Cole eyed his lawyer with icy resolve. "Maybe, but I need to know what she'll do."

CHAPTER THIRTEEN

EVER since Jen met Cole that fateful day over a month ago, she'd slept restlessly, if at all, her dreams worrisome, erotic, filled with images of him, of her, together. Since their marriage, those dreams had only become more fiery, impossible to put out of her thoughts.

Being near him at work had been haunting and painful in the extreme. Remaining married to him couldn't be more precarious, for her credibility as president or for her heart. So, why on earth did she resist going forward with the annulment?

On Friday night, exactly two weeks and one day after their wedding, she shored up the cracks in her courage and went to Cole's penthouse apartment. He had saved her from making the mistake of an unnecessary, loveless marriage, and she needed to thank him for that, at least. When she arrived a pleasant butler showed her to a comfortable room filled with oversize, casual furniture in earth tones. The agreeable scent of cedarwood and leather filled the air.

Too nervous to sit, Jen stood before a picture window looking out over the dusky environs of steel, stone and glass skyscrapers that was Dallas, a cultured city despite its Wild West image. A setting sun bathed the uppermost stories of the tallest buildings in dazzling light. *Like Cole's eyes.* She blanched at the comparison that had whipped in so quickly she hadn't been able to block it.

She closed her eyes, resting her forehead on the cool glass, struggling to defend the place in her heart where Cole had taken up stubborn residence. Why must every sight, every sound, every place she went, every song on the radio, remind her of the man who married her *only* to teach her a lesson?

"Well, if it isn't my bride…"

Jen whirled at the sound of Cole's voice.

"…so to speak," he drawled. Though his statement was civil, his inflection filled the room with scorn.

Good Lord! He was dressed formally, in a tuxedo. She'd taken great pains with her appearance, yet she suddenly felt dowdy and underdressed in beige linen trousers and a silk blouse. Clearly he was on his way to some fancy evening— probably a date. Her eyes skidded on their own to his left hand. His wedding band glimmered there, taunting her. Maybe he forgot he had it on, or more likely he'd slipped it back on his finger to intimidate and fluster her.

His jaw firmly set, he met her gaze with unfriendly eyes. His antagonism stung, filling her with renewed misery. She couldn't let it show, the slashing pain, the barrenness of loving a man who hated the sight of her.

Striding toward her, his face impassive, he extended an arm, exposing an impeccable margin of starched, white cuff. "Good evening. I didn't expect to see you. How may I be of service—now?"

Ouch! She managed not to wince at his pointed reference to all he'd done for her, but inwardly she cried out, *Do you want the knife back, or should I just leave it in my chest?*

His expression and demeanor were gravely polite, as though she were a total stranger there to solicit funds for some charity. His deliberate barb coupled with such sterile courtesy only added fresh hurt to her battered heart.

She found it difficult to speak. He was so handsome. When he drew near she could detect the scent that was his and his alone. Her damaged heart thrilled foolishly as she took him in, his hand extended, his expression serious. She knew he expected a cultivated perfunctory handshake. But her hands were so trembly, she couldn't chance it, so she laced her fingers together in a tight ball and commanded herself to settle down. She must try to appear as composed as he.

"Cole," she said, then cleared her throat to steady her voice before forging on. "I—I have a tendency to be determined and enthusiastic when going after a goal."

His eyebrows knit. Apparently he hadn't expected her to refuse his touch or start right in on some informational commentary. He crossed his arms and stared her down. "I see." His expression held a note of mockery. "Is that the whole speech?"

She shook her head. "No. I—er—what I'm trying to say is, in the past being determined and enthusiastic have been good business tactics, but this time I realize I went too far. I—I wanted to apologize."

His gaze roamed over her face in a drawn-out, tense pause before he spoke. "Finding a husband should not be a matter of business tactics, Miss Sancroft—excuse me, *Mrs. Barringer*." The emphasis on her married name made his implication clear—she hadn't begun the annulment proceedings.

That was a whole other subject, one she wanted badly to broach, but didn't dare. She knew what his response would be. A hearty, contemptuous laugh. She experienced a rush of sorrow and had to blink fiercely to hold back defeated tears.

"I accept your apology." He flicked a glance at his wristwatch, another undisguised confirmation that he was anxious to be rid of her. "Enjoy the presidency," he said. "You earned it."

The pseudo-compliment stung. She could only stare into his eyes, sparking with condemnation.

"I have to go," he said. "Is there anything else you wanted to tell me?"

Yes, yes! her mind screamed. *I love you! Isn't there any way we can work things out? Is there nothing about me you could find to like or admire?*

Another voice nudged her consciousness, slyly whispering, *Didn't you learn anything from all this, Jennifer? Love is illogical. You can't force someone to love you any more than you can make yourself stop loving a man who detests your motives for marriage almost as much as he hates the sight of you.*

She shuddered inwardly at the terrible truth, and shook her head. "No—nothing."

A shadow of some emotion crossed his face. She couldn't tell if it was annoyance or possibly even regret. Regret? She shook off the silliness. Of course, it was annoyance. "Then, I'll be going," he said. "Richard will see you out."

He turned, paused, seeming to have a thought. Slowly, he shifted to look at her. "Since you are my wife, then it follows that I am your husband—with all the rights and privileges." A sardonic, half-smile twisted his lips. "Stay married to me much longer, sweetheart, and there *will* be a honeymoon." Though spoken softly, Jen recognized the ever-present contempt in his eyes. Her emotions warred. Oh, how she wanted to share a honeymoon with this man. But the animosity in his eyes kept her mute. She could *not* survive his scornful laughter.

Crazy with yearning and defeat, she heard herself blurt, "I liked you better as a handyman!"

His scowl deepening, his gaze lingered on her for one more heartbeat before he pivoted away without comment. A few seconds later she heard the slam of a door.

Cole was gone.

She stood there numb, her protest echoing in her ears. She was mortified to have shouted at him. Hadn't she come to try to mend the rift between them? Even so, she had shouted the truth. Why couldn't J. C. Barringer be Cole Noone again? She would have given anything to return to those times when he had surprised her with iced tea or insisted she linger and eat a good meal. How she longed to listen to a French aria with him, share the antics of that silly, infatuated duck, or sit beside him in the moonlight, just listening to the rush of surf.

She heard someone clear his throat and her head shot up to see the butler standing in the living room entry. She wiped at a tear, and with as much poise as she could gather, allowed the manservant to escort her out of Cole's home.

The July night was warm, but Jen felt chilled through to her core. Loving a man who held her in utter contempt left a vast, frozen emptiness in her soul.

Monday morning Jen left on a business trip to California, relieved to be out from under Cole's smoldering stare. Her last act before leaving was to hire a lawyer to begin annulment proceedings. She didn't want Cole's contempt or his wealth. Though it broke her heart, she knew the only thing she could do to prove she had no greedy, ulterior motives was to give the man she loved his freedom.

On Friday, just before her return, her new secretary telephoned to inform her about an "executive budget meeting" to be held at the gulf house over the weekend. Unsettled, she reluctantly changed her return flight from Dallas to Corpus Christi so she could go straight to the beach property from the airport.

During her California trip, while tossing and turning each night, she had reluctantly come to the conclusion she must find another job, somewhere far away from Cole Barringer. She cared a great deal about D.A.A. and she loved Cole more than words could describe. Even so, the pain of being near him, witnessing the animosity in his eyes, was too horrific to endure, even for a presidency she had worked for so many years to achieve.

That evening, tired from a long day, she pulled her rental car to a stop in the beach house drive. Heated memories of Cole rushed back in sweet and torturous detail. She could see lights on in the house, but when she rang the bell no one came to the door. At first she was confused, then she just felt stupid. Had there been any other cars in the drive?

No. "They're out to dinner, you idiot," she muttered, fishing around in her purse for the key. For once her preoccupation with Cole had been a blessing, since it made her forget to return the key to corporate leasing.

She unlocked the door, thankful to have time alone to get her emotions under control before the others arrived. Unfortunately for her peace of mind, Cole would be in attendance, since only the CEO could call a meeting requiring her presence. She would have to find a private moment to relieve his mind about their impending annulment, as well as her decision to leave D.A.A. Both decisions had been the most soul-wrenching of her life, but she had no choice.

Closing the door behind her, she set down her suitcase, weary and heavy-hearted. She inhaled for strength, startled and saddened to note the house was permeated with his scent. How unjust! How cruel of the fates! Wasn't her heart ravaged enough without every breath reminding her of all she'd lost?

She sensed movement in the living room and glanced toward it. A man came to his feet before one of the wing chairs grouped in front of the windows. She blinked, not believing her eyes. He looked like Cole.

"Won't you come in?" he said, his handsomely sculptured features solemn.

Her throat went dry and she could only gape. Seeing him, standing there, rakishly good-looking and serious, broke her heart.

"Cole?" She was afraid her futile longing might be causing her to hallucinate the whole scene.

"Yes." He indicated the sofa at an angle to his chair. "Come in. Sit down," he said, quietly.

She was too confused to immediately react. "I—I thought everybody was out to dinner." She sensed a bout of mindless jabbering coming on and told herself to keep quiet.

"Come. Take a seat." He offered again, beckoning her

forward, while remaining on his feet as she cautiously moved from the entryway into the living room and rounded to the front of the couch. "Go on," he said, unsmiling. "Join me."

She sat down heavily, her legs having taken on the consistency of wet paper. "Am I early?" she asked, trying to appear business-like, though it was difficult. Before his sensuous, brilliant eyes, so direct and challenging, her hard-fought defenses melted like an ice cube in full sunshine. Fighting for composure, she folded her hands in her lap.

He took his seat, lounging there like a prince at his leisure. The table lamp beside his chair gave off a golden glow that accentuated his angular good looks. He wore beige trousers and a light blue polo shirt that brought out the blue in his eyes. His hair was casually mussed, as though by the sea breeze. She inhaled, an incongruous sense of peace washing over her at the very sight of him.

"You're right on time." Placing an elbow on the chair arm, he leaned toward her. "Tell me, Madam President, what do you feel is the most important trait in a spouse?"

The unexpected query disconcerted her. "What?" That had been one of the questions she'd asked in her husband hunt.

He angled his head inquiringly. "I mean, do you feel your spouse should be good with children? Would you prefer that he do the cooking? How do you feel about pets? Do you have any hobbies? If so, what are they and how much time do they take—an hour a day, three hours a week, all weekend?" He paused, one eyebrow rising as if to emphasize the gravity of his investigation.

Her heart sank. He was mocking her again! Would it never end? "Why are you doing this?" she asked, her voice ragged with humiliation.

His inquiring expression reverted to grim seriousness. "I thought this was the way you looked for a spouse."

It was a humbling, defeating feeling to have her foolishness thrown back at her this way, especially by Cole. She shook her head. "I know it was stupid." She sighed, her voice filled with anguish. "Haven't you made that point enough ways without humiliating me like this?"

"If you had known I was J. C. Barringer, what would you have done?" he asked, his wonderful eyes riveted on hers.

She was confused by his question. She searched his face, uncertain. It was hard to remain coherent this close to him. His scent swirled about her, enticing, beguiling, even in the face of his severe attitude. Flustered, she crossed her arms and looked away. "I—I'd have left the house, I guess."

He was quiet for so long she couldn't help but look at him. Reluctantly, she admired the way the lamplight made the fringe of his lashes cast long shadows on his cheeks.

"You wouldn't have tried to cozy up to me?" he asked, sounding dubious.

His assumption that she would be so devious made her temper flair. Just because she'd been foolish, thinking she could find a mate by advertising, in no way meant she would be so calculating and corrupt. Her anger billowed. "You *did* get the annulment papers from my lawyer, didn't you? And the document that frees you from *any* financial obligations?"

His nod was grave and slow. "And your wedding ring."

"Yes—well then…" At the reminder, she covered her naked ring finger with her other hand, her sorrow almost overwhelming her ability to remain outwardly composed. "You have your answer." Deeply wounded, she swallowed hard and wiped at a humiliating tear. She didn't want him to glimpse even that tiny display of her utter wretchedness.

"Do I?" he queried.

She'd fixed her gaze on her knotted hands in her lap. But at his odd question she flicked her attention back to him. He removed an envelope from beneath his chair. As she stared, perplexed, he pulled from it several sheets of paper. Placing them on top of the envelope in his lap, he looked at her. "Why exactly do you want the annulment?"

That question hit her like a blow. The last thing on earth she wanted was that annulment. She stared as his eyes lingered on her face, provoking, enticing, coaxing from her things she didn't want to admit.

"Why exactly do you want the annulment, Jennifer?" he repeated more gently. Somewhere in the back of her brain, an answer was forming without her consent. She began to fear losing control, blurting out the terrible truth. Those eyes, so cunningly alluring, so devastatingly persuasive, could lay waste to the hardest-fought determination.

She sat rigidly, hardly able to breathe, battling to keep from spilling out her heart and soul. All the while her defenses crumbled around her, like chalk battered by a velvet-clad hammer.

Suddenly she could no longer hold in the awful truth, and it poured from her, an emotional, remorseful confession. "I *don't* want the annulment. I love you, Cole," she whispered, her voice breaking. "I know now that for a marriage to work it needs two people who are in love. You don't love me. You don't even like me." She pressed her fists to her temples. A harrowing headache pounded in her forehead from the screaming inside her brain, telling her, *Shut up! Shut up! Shut up, you lovesick fool!*

Her stomach pitched and rolled. She felt ill, shamed, but she couldn't stop herself. "You don't trust me and because of your history I can't blame you! That's why I'm getting the annulment—because it's what *you* want." She vaulted up, mortified to her soul. "I'm giving notice. I'm quitting. I can't be near you, can't see you every day. It—it breaks my heart." She spun away to make her escape.

He grasped her wrist, holding her captive. "You're not leaving, yet."

When he compelled her to face him, she tried desperately to stifle a sob with the back of her hand. But she could no longer staunch forlorn tears. "Why?" she cried. "What more do you want from me? Haven't I been humiliated enough?"

"Please," he said. "Sit down." Without releasing her wrist, he nodded toward the couch. His message was unmistakable; he was giving her no choice. "Just one more thing."

She felt vacant, spent, all emotions washed away with her painful revelation. What was there left of her that he could take away? Allowing a hopeless sigh to escape her lips, she sat down feebly, wrecked.

His confining hand slid from her wrist to hold her hand. "That was the answer I needed to hear."

She sat there in an all-consuming whirlpool of gloom and despair. Not comprehending, she stared blankly at his hand holding hers. What had he said? It didn't make sense.

"Jennifer..." He gently squeezed her fingers. "Look at me."

Drained, without hope or strength of will, she did as he asked. What she saw stunned her. He was smiling—not a mocking grin nor a twisted sneer, but a gentle-hearted curving of his lips that stole her breath.

"Do you remember I told you my mother used my father to get a promotion of sorts?"

She nodded, feeling dazed, confused.

"My mother is Adrianne Bourne, the actress. She used her pregnancy with me, used my father's power and connections, to get what she wanted—a Hollywood career."

That revelation shocked Jen. She'd heard of Adrianne Bourne, even seen some of her old movies—a stunning woman with unearthly, iridescent eyes. So she was Cole's mother, scarring him deeply with her egocentric greed.

He released her hand and retrieved the pages from his lap. "These are the annulment papers. When I got them, I finally allowed myself to admit I'm hopelessly in love with you," he whispered. "The fact that you don't want anything from me proves you're not the kind of woman I led myself to believe." He tore the document in half and dropped the pieces to the floor.

Leaning forward, he took her hand again. Raising it to

his lips, he brushed her knuckles with a kiss. "The last thing in the world I want is to watch you walk away—Mrs. Barringer."

He surprised her by moving from the chair and kneeling before her.

"I was crazy in love with you when I married you, Jennifer. I didn't want to be, didn't want to take the vows seriously, but I had no choice. I think I fell in love with you the first moment I saw you." Reaching into his pocket he drew out something and held it up for her to see. It was her wedding ring. "Please take this back." The gentle flame she saw in his eyes awed her. "I would never have given it to you if I didn't want you to keep it forever."

Could she really believe the beauty, the sincerity, of his softly spoken vow? His gaze traveled over her face, searched her eyes. "We all do foolish things, darling, but that day we exchanged marriage vows wasn't one of them." Their eyes locked and her heart took a joyous leap. "I'm still wearing your ring," he said.

Startled, Jen's glance skidded to his left hand. It was there!

"Don't leave me," he murmured. The beauty of what she saw made her heart ache beneath her breast. His vulnerability was a precious gift, one that wrapped her in an invisible warmth.

She smiled tremulously and touched his cheek. "I adore you," she whispered. "I'll never leave you. Not ever."

The radiant splendor that burst to life in his eyes affected her deeply, filling her with a dizzying, boundless joy. She knew it was a sight she would recall often, and cherish.

He slid the ring on her trembling finger, then kissed the palm of her hand, gently, sweetly.

Her wildly beating heart was the only sound she could hear. The intensity of his earnestness and his passion sizzled through her. Cole Barringer truly loved her. Miracle of miracles, he honestly *loved* her! She threw herself into his arms, crying out in a half laugh, half sob, "Oh, oh, darling! I can't believe it."

"Believe it, my love," he whispered. She was aware of nothing else but his heat, his strength and the glorious truth of his love, shimmering there in his eyes. "Jen, sweetheart, you don't need to quit your job. I'm not going to be active CEO any longer, since you can handle things just fine without me."

Her exultant emotions tumbled down at the reminder of her presidency. "I—I can't stay on as president. If we announce our marriage nobody will believe I got the job on merit."

He grinned, pulling her down to the carpet and hugging her close. "Oh, yes they will. When Ruthie got back from Houston and found out who I really was, she laughed so long and loud the story couldn't be kept quiet. Everybody knows you had no idea I was J. C. Barringer when you married me."

He kissed her nose, nibbled her ear, then met her gaze, his expression serious. "Besides, if my reputation for impartiality weren't indisputable enough..." He gently touched her face, as though she were a holy shrine. "...no one can dispute what you've already done in the few weeks since you took over. I've heard enough praise from your staff to be sure they feel you were the right choice, married to me or not."

He kissed her with all the sweet passion her erotic dreams had promised. A quiver of delight surged through her. "Cole, darling, I'm glad you feel I can handle the presidency by myself. But I promise you, in no *other* area of my life can I do without you."

The love shining in his eyes spoke volumes. She knew from what he'd told her of his father and his own feelings on the subject of marriage, that he didn't commit to a woman casually, or for any reason other than true, abiding love. That knowledge brought tears to her eyes and she kissed him softly, slowly, murmuring, "I love you—forever and ever." Her vow to hold his heart with utmost care was unconditional and without hesitation.

Their passion built in a series of unhurried, shivery kisses, a pleasurable prelude to the honeymoon Jen had lost hope of ever experiencing.

She had a scary thought, and pressed at his chest. "But—but Cole, what if the others get here and we're...we're..." She blushed.

"Making wild love?" he finished for her, his tongue teasing the hollow of her throat. Lowering his head, he nipped at the top button on her blouse, magically unfastening it. "No one else is coming, sweetheart." His warm, moist breath caressed her breasts. "Honeymooners don't need company."

He lifted his gaze to hers, his eyes full of the devotion she had longed to see. Her heart soared and she cuddled his head to her. "Make love to me, Cole!" She kissed his silky hair, inhaling deeply of his clean, male scent. "Make wild love to me, right here. Right now."

His soft sigh tickled sensitive flesh. "Whatever the lady wants." The lusty nip of his teeth on her lower lip sent a sensual thrill rushing through her. His hand slipped beneath her skirt to skim upward along her thigh.

His fingers, his lips, sought out pleasure points to surprise and delight. Before long her breathy sighs became moans of desire.

Their lovemaking was wild and wickedly wonderful—a soul-blending covenant. On that very special honeymoon weekend, Cole and his bride joyfully, freely—and almost ceaselessly—celebrated their love, a blissful dawning of the heaven on earth they would share.

magazine

♥————————————————— **quizzes**

Is he the one? What kind of lover are you? Visit the **Quizzes** area to find out!

♥————————————— **recipes for romance**

Get scrumptious meal ideas with our **Recipes for Romance.**

♥———————————————— **romantic movies**

Peek at the **Romantic Movies** area to find Top 10 Flicks about First Love, ten Supersexy Movies, and more.

♥————————————————— **royal romance**

Get the latest scoop on your favorite royals in **Royal Romance.**

♥—————————————————————— **games**

Check out the **Games** pages to find a ton of interactive romantic fun!

♥————————————————— **romantic travel**

In need of a romantic rendezvous? Visit the **Romantic Travel** section for articles and guides.

♥—————————————————————— **lovescopes**

Are you two compatible? Click your way to the **Lovescopes** area to find out now!

 HARLEQUIN®

makes any time special—online...

If you enjoyed what you just read,
then we've got an offer you can't resist!

Take 2 bestselling love stories FREE!

Plus get a FREE surprise gift!

$ **Saving Money** $
Has Never Been
This Easy!

**Just fill out and send in this form from any
October, November and December 2002 books
and we will send you a coupon booklet worth a
total savings of $20.00 off future purchases of
Harlequin and Silhouette books in 2003.**

Yes! It's that easy!

**i accept your incredible offer!
Please send me a coupon booklet:**

Name (PLEASE PRINT)

Address   Apt. #

City   State/Prov.   Zip/Postal Code

**In a typical month, how many
Harlequin and Silhouette novels do you read?**
❏ **0-2**   ❏ **3+**

097KJKDNC7   097KJKDNDP

Please send this form to:
In the U.S.: Harlequin Books, P.O. Box 9071, Buffalo, NY 14269-9071
In Canada: Harlequin Books, P.O. Box 609, Fort Erie, Ontario L2A 5X3

Allow 4-6 weeks for delivery. Limit one coupon booklet per household. Must be
postmarked no later than January 15, 2003.

HARLEQUIN®
Makes any time special®

Silhouette®
Where love comes alive™

A brand-new title by
Betty Neels

With more than 134 novels to her name,
international bestselling author **Betty Neels**
has left a legacy of wonderful romances
to enjoy, cherish and keep.

Curl up this winter and enjoy
the enchantment of a Christmas
never to be forgotten, with
the magic of a mistletoe marriage...

THE FORTUNES
OF FRANCESCA

Professor Marc van der Kettener has been
a helping hand since he met Francesca—but
now he's proposed! Francesca is torn: is Marc
simply helping her out of a tight spot again,
or has he really fallen in love?

On sale December 2002 (#3730)

Don't miss this tantalizing Christmas treat from

EMOTIONALLY EXHILARATING!